The Lion and I

by Ariana D.L.

Paperback ISBN: 978-1-66781-056-0
eBook ISBN: 978-1-66781-057-7

"History will judge what I am fighting for."

Ahmad Shah Massoud

Content

My "faal" [1]

"The nightingale with drops of his hearts blood had nourished the red rose.
Then came a wind
And pulling at the bows in envious mood
A hundred thorns at his heart entwined

Like a parrot crunching sugar –
good seemed the world to me that could not stay
The wind of death that blew my hopes away

Light of mine eyes and harvest of my heart
Mine at least in changeless memories
Oh, when he found it easy to depart
He left the harder pilgrimage to me

Oh, camel driver – though the cortege starts
For God's sake, help me pick up my fallen load
And pity be my comrade of the road

I had not castled, and the time is gone
What should I play? On the chequered floor of night and day?
Death won the game
Forlorn and careless now – I can lose no more!"

Hafiz

Translated by Getrude Bell, an eminent British scholar and writer of the 19th and early 20th century.

---

[1] those who read the Persian Sufi poet Hafiz, often open his books at a random page and consider the poem they open a prediction of their fate. This is called a "faal". When I learned of Massoud in 2003 and started reading Hafiz poems, this was the poem I opened at random.

The first time ever
I saw your face [2]

Why this book?

Someone once said: "Love and death have one thing in common: they often come uninvited".

In 2003, through the medium of television, I had been overwhelmed by a face. The face of Ahmad Shah Massoud, the "Lion of Panjshir"[3], the legendary Afghan resistance leader.

A face so charismatic, that it spoke to me volumes about the man behind it. As if through some secret communication I knew who he was, I knew his character – I knew that he had been a wonderful man and human being – strong, yet humane.

There is no rational explanation for this as I had not heard of him before, had never met him before, and no one was there to shape my opinion about him. What made it more amazing was the fact that I would be confirmed all this face had communicated to me later when I met various people who had known him, who had been close to him.

---

[2] Song originally recorded by Roberta Flack
[3] Ahmad Shah, nom de guerre, Massoud, *1953-✝2001

So, what did I do? With my deep emotions which had come out of nowhere, it seemed? Which had literally taken a hold on me within one hour?

What did I do when faced with the abyss of him being gone forever? What did I do when I realised, I was attaching my emotions to someone I could never meet, a phantom, a mirage, a dead man?

I contacted people who knew him, who had been close to him to learn more.

I collected everything I could find on him – photos, reports, articles, videos.

I bought a ticket to his country, risking life and limb to cry at his tomb and to work there for his memory

and

I wrote my dream down.

The following is a fictional story, yet it is based on historic facts and actual persons, places, and events as I have learned about them in personal experience, literature, and conversations with people during my eleven years in Afghanistan. Everyone and everything is real, except Ariana. She was placed on the scene, which is why it is fiction.

The story does not mean to give a consecutive account of political and military events, but it is set against their historically correct backdrop. I am not claiming each minute detail to be accurate, but I have tried my best.

This story reflects who I believe Ahmad Shah Massoud was - based on my intuition and what people have told me about him.

This story tells of my dream to meet the man of my dreams. It is a dream-brought-to-paper which could not have materialised in the real world. For many reasons.

It was a catalyst, my means to emotional sanity in a time of emotional turmoil.

The title of my book is reminiscent of the 19th century life-story of Anna Leonowens, which was fictionalised in the book "Anna and the king of Siam" and the movies "The King and I" and in a later version "Anna and the King".

While Anna Leonowens did live in Siam for six years, working at the royal court as the tutor to the king's children, the romantic leanings in the book and the movies are fiction. But the sentiment behind them is the same as in my story: a man from a far-removed culture falls for a western woman due to her temperament and love for his country.

My story does not mean to offend, much rather it is born out of the deepest respect I have ever felt for anyone. It is a homage written in ink of pain. And I hope that this sentiment is shared by readers from all cultures.

Some people have not agreed to have their name used in my story or I simply decided not to reveal them directly. Their real names have been replaced by pseudonyms. However, resemblance to persons living or dead is fully intended.

How to catch a dream

It was a warm Friday evening in Singapore, in July 1997, the type which makes you feel you have an endless weekend ahead. A nice breeze was blowing, and the sky was dotted with fluffy clouds. One met with friends, had a few drinks, banished all office-worries.

I have always loved the twilight hour in the tropics – this fast half hour of the setting sun in an often-friendly sky. It gives everything the warmest glow and even a city landscape like this will light up in warm colours.

A friend had rung me a few days prior to tell me about an exhibition – photographs from Iran to Afghanistan. She could not recall the photographer's name but since this was my area of interest, I agreed to meet her for the opening. I was on time of course, while she was not, so I had time to look around.

They had done beautiful jobs with renovating these old Chinese Shop Houses – restored to their old splendour in the most vibrant colours and architectural detail. The Straits Chinese were colourful people – as colourful as their mixed Malay and Chinese heritage.

Their forbears were Chinese who had migrated to Malaya and settled in the Straits of Malacca and Straits of Singapore. Intermarrying and mixing with the Malays their dress had changed to colourful Baju Kebayas and Sarongs, their cooking had become Malay, but is a unique blend with Chinese food. The spices are Southeast Asian, while their dishes often contain pork.

It was these traders then who built these two-storey shop houses, decorated with colourful ornaments, each in its own pastel shade. Today these beauties are confined to "conservation areas" where they have become expensive boutiques, small restaurants and more.

The setting evening sun gave the buildings even more depth. Folding my arms, I walked down Tanjong Pagar Road. From one restaurant to a bridal salon, passing by posh small IT firms who could afford the enormous rentals these places commanded.

At the corner was a coffee shop with old men having their "thé" and "kopi" – like they do every day, everywhere across Singapore.

"Kopi siew dai" [black coffee with sugar] jelled the coffee shop helper less than a metre away from my ear, to ensure that the drinks-stall owner heard him. While pondering the question which had been nagging at me for years, whether it was a pre-requisite to be almost deaf to own a drinks stall in a Singaporean coffee shop, I decided to sit down at a corner table.

I could hear the tell-tale clacking of a metal spoon being spun quickly inside a mug to disperse the sugar sitting at the bottom of a Thé Tarik ["pull tea"]. This tea gets its name from the fact that it is poured into a mug from about twenty centimetres away, thereby cooling it and creating a typical froth. An old Indian Muslim man at the neighbouring table had just been put the sweet drink in front of him. Slurping with content, the wrinkled little man settled back in his plastic chair.

Coffee shops have always been the place where the soul of Singapore steps out of hiding. Here they refuse to "speak

Mandarin"[4] – the Chinese dialects, Singlish and Malay are the lingua franca. Politics are made around these coffee shop tables – even in, almost, one-party Singapore. "The gaament" ["the government"] is blamed for many things but still always voted back into power.

Personally, I never found it boring here – there is far more to see and know than the locals will want you to believe. Far more profoundness in culture and history than the new world – where many Singaporeans' dreams lie – can ever produce.

After some ten minutes I got up and when reaching back at the exhibition venue its poster caught my eye. Only now did I realize the photographer's name. From one moment to the other my Friday-after-work-mind sprang into action: J.B.? J.B.!

If one name was eternally edged into my mind it was his – French Iranian dissident photographer, famous for his work for various international magazines but most of all friend of my love and hero: Ahmad Shah Massoud – legendary Afghan resistance fighter and lately turned Afghanistan's last hope against the advancing Taliban as the de facto leader of the Northern Alliance.

Everything connected to Massoud makes my heart beat faster. So suddenly I started kicking my heels – where was my friend? Did people always have to be late?

Finally, she arrived mumbling an obligatory excuse.

---

[4] A Singapore government campaign which encourages the local ethnic Chinese to abandon their dialects in favour of the standard Mandarin

16

Pushing open the wooden doors with their Peranakan[5] stain glass inlay we stepped into the shop-house, which was already beaming with people and voices. The walls were dotted with photographs the colour palette of which would have been attraction enough – even without looking closely.

We stepped in at the right moment; somebody sounded a glass and the voices died down. A lady stepped up to a makeshift podium and announced J.B., giving a brief overview of his persona. She did not touch on his special Afghanistan connections much – it was a fact little known to the public particularly in these parts.

Then J.B. himself took the microphone. I barely recognized him without his pakul[6].

I had never realised that he was almost bald. It felt as if Massoud himself was speaking – that's how excited I was. While he was speaking my mind started to race. I had to talk to him, I had to see if I could get together with him separately just to talk about Massoud, get a personal account from a friend, learn whatever possible of the man I had been dreaming about to be close to for years. I had all Massoud's publicly available photographs, all stories, all accounts, all footage - everything about him.

I had read up about his campaigns and victory against the Soviets as well as his early activism against the Communist Afghan government in the late 1970s. I had suffered with him through the turmoil of the past few years, which brought the war-wracked country to its knees. It was sometimes hard to come by information but digging always reaped results. I had read of how he was the only commander of the various Mujahedin factions who managed to cut across tribal lines, organise the region he controlled politically and socially to

---

[5] Another name for the Straits Chinese
[6] an Afghan flat, woolen hat.

the benefit of the people. From all I had read he was an extraordinary leader with extraordinary charisma. An intelligent, cultured and educated individual.

From the first photograph on I had been spellbound; to me his appearance spoke volumes about his character; and this package has been irresistible to me ever since.

The more I had read and learned the more I had fallen in love. If I had ever had the chance to work for and with him, I would have jumped at it, forsaking everything else.

My mind was only halfway concentrating on the photographs as I went around with my friend. But beautiful they were – J.B. was a gifted photographer. Particularly, I felt, he knew how to capture light, producing the most amazing depth.

And then I saw it – one of five photos featuring Massoud. I suddenly knew what to do. I told my friend to wait around – I'd be back.

Quite experienced in events which required you to hold on to a glass of alcohol for an hour I swiftly grabbed one off a waiter's tray and moved in J.B.'s direction. I felt like a cat patiently stalking its pray. Then, my window of opportunity: a rather robust gentleman moved out of the circle and seizing the moment of silence between J.B. and the beleaguering crowd I made my move. "Excuse me, J.B.", I said, trying not to sound too excited. "I am sorry to bother you. My name is Ariana, and I was wondering if I can ask you a question." Looking my way, he smiled and replied in his unmistakable soft voice and French accent.

"Yes of course. Good to meet you."

"Is it possible to buy some of your photographs" I continued, encouraged by his warm response. "Absolutely – please let the counter know and they will get it for you. Various sizes are available."

A potential conversation killer had crept in – this could be the end of my cleverly conceived manoeuvre. So, I quickly added: "You know, I just need to get your Massoud photos. I like to believe that I have them all, but I must be mistaken" I tried to quip.

That did the trick. I had his full attention now. "Really" he asked "why?"

"Massoud is my hero." I replied rather bluntly, unable to express in a short sentence what he means to me. "I would give everything to meet him" I added lowering my eyes into my glass.

"He is indeed a wonderful person," J.B. continued. "It is always good to meet people who seem to understand his personality and character."

"Thank you." I looked up again "you know, I have to confess something to you: the reason why I approached you were not those photographs – even though of course I must buy them – but I was wondering if you could make time in your busy schedule to meet outside of this. I would just like to know everything about Massoud, every possible detail ... don't worry, I'm not a journalist or something else covert." After it was out, I felt like a little child, having laid bare my feelings to someone I had never met.

"I really appreciate your feelings and your interest, but I am on a very tight schedule. I am flying out of Singapore tomorrow morning."

"I completely understand, and I am really sorry to be a nuisance, but this would mean such a lot to me – you have no idea! Please, J.B., just one hour – I meet you in your hotel lobby, drinks on me ..."

I must have looked at him with great desperation as he finally agreed to meet me later that night in his hotel.

We met at 11.00 – when I left the hotel it was 3am.

I could not tare myself away from all J.B. had to tell and he was quite happy to share whatever he knew. Many things moved me to tears at the thought of such a wonderful individual – how I yearned to meet him!

And then it happened: J.B. mentioned – casually almost – that he was going to attempt to meet Massoud yet again later that year with a camera crew to document for the National Geographic Channel the Northern Alliance's efforts to defeat the Taliban after they had taken Kabul in September last year.

It was 1am and I had been up for 18 hours but at that moment I felt awake as if I had just woken from a ten-hour sleep. For the second time that night my mind started racing:

How long did he want to go? One month.

All plans finalized yet? No – final permit from Massoud pending.

How was he planning on getting there? Via Dushanbe, Tajikistan, and a helicopter flight into Northern Alliance territory.

"Until September there will be huge amounts of preparation work; you know the first time when I met Massoud in 1982 we had to undertake a 3-months track across the Hindu Kush to get into his territory – that was of course in Soviet times; a quite different ballpark altogether, but ...

"J.B.," I interrupted him as my racing mind faded out his voice, "you will straight away send me to a mental institution but here it goes:

Can I come along?"

J.B.'s jaw dropped and for a second there he lost his train of thought. After he recovered, he looked at me

"What? You mean come along on this assignment? What for?"

"To meet Massoud!"

At that moment I felt a tinge of irritation – had I not demonstrated that I was ready to do everything to meet this man?

"And also" I continued to soften my approach, "I have been thinking for the longest time to write some sort of 'front line diary' and try to sell it …". The latter I had made up on the spot to give my crazy notion a serious backdrop. But the more I thought about it later the more sense it made. Yes, I could go there and write my first or only ever-published article …

"Well," I could see J.B. struggling with his words "personally I find it is very dangerous for someone inexperienced and even more so for a woman. So, I would discourage it".

"But I will be with you and your crew – you are experienced, and I will do everything you tell me."

At that moment I was catapulted back to my childhood: 'Dad, please, let me do this, I will be well behaved and do everything you tell me. I won't be stubborn or naughty.'

J.B. looked at me half concerned, half amused.

"Alright. Personally, I'd be ok with it, but I can't make a final decision on that. There will be insurance concerns with

National Geographic and once that is passed, we will have to convince Massoud."

"Of course, I have to depend on you to sell me well and I'll sign a waiver, if necessary." I quipped with excitement seeing my dream moving closer than ever before.

15th August 1997

My phone rang at 11pm. I had already gone to bed. It was J.B. from France. I had not heard from him for three weeks and my hopes of doing this trip with him had started to fade.

"Ariana, I don't know whether to congratulate you or give you my condolences: National Geographic as well as Massoud have given permission to bring you along!

Please make your travel arrangements to Dushanbe yourself. I will send you all details on when to arrive there, what hotel to check into and so forth." I gasped for air – I sat upright in my bed – I could not help but to let go a yell to release the tension which had built up from the second I saw J.B.'s caller ID on my phone.

There went my sleep for the rest of the night!

16th September 1997

4.00 am Singapore time. I boarded the Aeroflot flight with stopover in New Delhi to Dushanbe, Tajikistan, accompanied by a rather large duffle bag, my laptop computer, my disc man, a photo camera, and no sane idea of what I was actually doing on this flight.

I had arrived at Changi airport two hours early, unable to sleep, I left my flat at 1.00 am. A mix of excitement and stress

22

filled my stomach. I left for unfamiliar ground in every respect.

10.00 am Dushanbe local time. I had just stepped down from the plane in the Tajik capital. The first notion that hit me was how all these communist-influenced countries from Russia to China still featured the same sad airports and buildings, the same rain-washed cityscapes. Even after close to a decade of the breakup of the Soviet Union.

Luckily of course this was not my destination, but just a springboard to where my heart had dragged me: Afghanistan.

From the airport I made my way to the Vladimir Hotel in downtown Dushanbe where I was to meet J.B. and the camera crew. Later that afternoon we were scheduled – weather permitting – to be airlifted into Northern Alliance territory by the only – Russian – MI17 helicopter in their possession.

J.B. had already arrived that same morning and I met him in the lobby. He looked nervous.

"What is the problem?"

"Our crew may be delayed by several hours due to a strike at Munich airport. If they don't arrive well before nightfall, we can't board the helicopter. We need to take off latest one hour before sunset to reach there shortly before sundown. Anything else may spell disaster by crashing into a mountain."

The whole thing did not sound re-assuring but now we all had reached a point of no return and at this moment there was nothing else to do but wait. So, we left a note at the reception for our crew that we would be back in two to three hours at the latest.

To pass the time we made our way on foot to downtown Dushanbe. The downtown area was far nicer than the initial impression I got when driving in from the airport. We stopped at a small traditional-looking restaurant that served something I would have called "murtabak", as it resembled the doughy pancake the Indian-Muslim community serves in Singapore; there they stuff it with mutton, vegetables, egg or even sardine. This one, however, came only with mutton stuffing or plain and was so oil saturated that I literally felt fresh pimples popping. But I did not mind at this stage because it was delicious and at the same time I had not eaten since flying out of Singapore – Aeroflot was not going to win a culinary award with their menu.

After our meal J.B., who had visited here before and was familiar with the town area, showed me the main streets and the main mosque. The mosque's architecture was unlike anything I had ever seen – the most beautiful turquoise and many other brilliant colours of inlay work. I wanted to go inside but was disappointed by J.B.:

"Non-Muslims are not allowed inside at all, I am afraid. Something I have always resented about certain streams of the Muslim faith."

"I know - same," I said "some mosques in Singapore are equally intolerant. That is why I never go. Do you know, though, that I love the prayer call? I learned to love it in Turkey. It is so soothing."

Instead, we sat down in the courtyard of the mosque.

"Do you know, J.B., that Massoud's impact on me goes so far that I have gained new respect for Islam, particularly the Sufis. Just the fact that he loves Hafiz and Rumi and other Sufi poets made me read some of their poems and I discovered

24

the profound religious knowledge Sufis have. The West labelled them "mystics", but I believe there were true saints among them, people who truly new God."

"Yes, I agree, truly wise men were among the Sufis. Sufism is a much softer and more pleasing version of Islam, more integrating than all other sects.

You know I have met other foreigners who admired Massoud, but I have not come across anyone with such deep feelings for him. You give the impression that you have grasped the various levels of his personality before you even met him. That is amazing."

"He spoke to me from the first time I learned about him, when I first saw his face, I knew that this is an extraordinary individual" I smiled at him.

J.B. smiled back at me, nodding in understanding.

At two in the afternoon, we returned to the hotel and were pleased to learn that our crew had arrived by now. Furthermore, the weather had cleared very nicely so it appeared that this was going to be it and indeed at five o'clock we got word that the helicopter was about to meet us in the designated spot just south of the city where we all had already gathered.

I am not an expert on air-traffic devices, but when the old MI 17, captured from the Soviets at some point, had landed, I did not feel too reassured. Were we sure that this rather patched-up looking machine would get us there? But what was the point of questioning anything? I was going to Afghanistan, for heaven's sake, one had to take whatever came along. It probably would get worse from here.

As we took off into the night, for the first time in my life I had no idea of what lay ahead, whether I would be disappointed, excited, or even killed. I was flying into a vacuum, into a warzone. But I did not care. I had arrived at my destination – if I could not fulfil this dream, I might as well die. Meeting Massoud was the only real dream I ever had, meeting the man I had fallen for was all I had truly in my heart. Everything else came second.

Fully aware of that situation I had left a blank slate behind in Singapore. I had pre-paid 3 months of rent and told my landlady if she did not hear from me by December to rent out the flat to someone else. I had paid up all credit card debts and settled all other outstanding situations.

Even on the relationship front I wanted to be very clear with my fiancé why I went there. I wanted him to be aware of my feelings for another man – however crazy it might have sounded. In other words, I left the book of love open - to be continued or not. Everything was better than a lie. In this respect of course I left only question marks behind – he saw it as a break-up and did not understand what was going on. There was no point in explaining because admittedly the thought was too crazy to finish; rather, I was afraid to finish it so that I would not be disappointed if it did not come true. "It"? What was "it"? I could not even answer that!

Yet it was my heart, which was driving me to do this. Three months later he would tell me in a phone call that it was over, that he had been introduced to another girl.

The sun was setting fast, spilling his orange and red colour palette over the most incredible mountain scenery I had ever seen. Some of the highest altitudes were still or already snow caped.

Our pilot became worried about the fading light. Eventually though, after a one-and-a-half-hour flight across the Hindu Kush we touched down at the helicopter landing spot in the Panjshir Valley, near the village of Jangalak. The spot was only lit up by car headlights on high beam parked in a circle to accommodate the landing helicopter.

We were met by Massoud's men who then brought us to the guesthouse of the Northern Alliance in the village of Astana where we were assigned to different rooms. Purged on a slope overlooking the valley, it gives a scenic view onto the mountains and the river below. The mountains at that time of the year were bare, brown in colour, while the river's floodplain was green and full of life.

I had been given a room with two beds – far too spacious for one person. It looked out over the big terrace of the guesthouse. The whole building was laid out with fitted carpets and knotted rugs. We had water and electricity supply only for several hours a day when they ran the diesel generator. Being spoiled from countries with a functioning electricity grid this takes getting used to, but after a while one works around these things. I had experienced a similar situation during my studies in the Beijing University in 1992 when the showers could only be used for two hours in the morning and evening. This university was the most prestigious one in China at the time, and such hours were considered very generous. In other establishments they had to make due with less, even with limited electricity and heating.

The guesthouse featured a lounge with sofas where the walls were covered in wooden panels. This room had three long windows, one of which with a wide windowsill. These windows gave a fantastic view onto the scenery.

There was a dining room, too, with a large table which could sit twenty people comfortably. Not only did guests take their meals there but this was also the makeshift cabinet room of the displaced Rabbani government after it had to flee the Taliban capturing Kabul in September 1996.

Massoud had not returned to Panjshir and was only announced for two days later, so the next day there was nothing much to do but wait around, explore the beautiful valley, and wait again. That gave our camera crew the opportunity to shoot lots of footage which could be used later in various places in the documentary.

Located some two hours' drive north of Kabul in the foothills of the Hindukush, the Panjshir Valley is a fairly narrow gorge framed by bare mountains. In parts it is wider than in others. It is one of the most serene places one will find in the whole of Afghanistan. The Panjshir River is one of many fast-flowing water arms in the country and has wild rapids in places. It has a very fertile flood plain where all its famous fruit are grown. About two hundred villages dot the valley, most of which were destroyed during the Soviet invasion and particularly "Panjshir VII", the seventh operation by the Soviets directed against the valley to "smoke out" the resistance. There would be two more attempts to come, but these, too, failed.

The villages have been rebuilt ever since – yet traces of this incredible destruction can still be seen, and at that time one would find the most haunting reminders of it everywhere: many burned out Soviet tanks. Later, up to 2010, most were removed and turned into scrap metal.

From the moment I stepped out of my room the next morning onto that terrace and looked at the incredible beauty spread before me, I was spell-bound. I loved this place before I had even walked out of the house. In some places that happens to you. There is an instant connection, an instant feeling of "home" and serenity. For me, looking back, everything fell into place from the first day I stepped into Afghanistan.

Wherever we walked I was of course the centre of attention. I was not the only European person here, but I was certainly the only European woman. So, as we made our way around, children would follow me and stare. Women could either not be spotted or were passing by covered from head to toe so I could not make out whether they looked at me or not.

Everyone of Massoud's men was very hospitable, seeing to our every need.

Being the only women among all those men I kept as low a profile as possible. Nobody would address me anyway even on matters concerning me. J.B. was the one to reply to such questions. I observed this with partial amusement as none of the men seemed hostile. They just applied their cultural training – whether one approved of that or not.

Only when – as described later – Massoud himself openly spoke to me and treated me as an equal was my profile raised instantly. Massoud's wider circle, which prior to that had treated me with distant politeness, was now at my service – still reserved but with notable difference and personal interaction.

Amir Sahib[7]

The ultimate moment had finally arrived. Two days after our arrival Massoud had sent word that he was going to meet us at the same spot where we had landed at the Panjshir River. It was at 5 o'clock in the afternoon when J.B. and I had positioned ourselves on the right bank of the river when Massoud's helicopter came into view. At this place the Panjshir River, just opposite the guesthouse, is wide and calm.

Just seeing him perhaps two hundred metres away coming down the steps of the helicopter as the dust settled, made my stomach revolt, I felt it close with excitement – at that moment I could not have swallowed one bite of food. I turned to J.B.:

"This is him, isn't it? I can't believe that I am actually going to meet him! Thank you so much for bringing me here!"

"You are welcome!" J.B. smiled, amused at my excitement.

J.B. was in his element: he had fixed a long-range lens to his camera and started firing away. When I later watched the close-up footage, our cameraman was taking, I saw Massoud's beautiful smile as he greeted his men.

When he reached us, his eyes immediately found J.B. and the two old friends embraced, greeting each other with "salaam aleikum" followed by the rather long-winded string of

---

[7] Honorary title for Massoud, literally meaning "Sir Leader"

Persian pleasantries which is custom to exchange if friends have not met for a while.

I had put on a dark-pink chador[8], a loose, knee-length beige kurta, jeans, boots with some heel and had been careful to put on the nicest "kajal" [Indian eye coal] stroke I could master. After all, I wanted to look my best from the start.

And then it was my turn – J.B. led Massoud to where I was standing and introduced me to him in Persian.

"This is Ariana."

"Salaam aleikum" He greeted me.

"Waleikum a salaam, Sahib" I replied, at the same time taking down my sunglasses and bringing my right hand to my chest. This is the customary way in this part of the world to greet each other and normally no physical contact between an unrelated man and a woman was allowed. So, I was expecting no shaking of hands.

But Massoud decided otherwise – he offered his hand to me.

His grip was firm, and for a quick second he looked me straight in the eyes.

At this moment my perception was reduced to slow motion in my memory, and I clearly remember his movement towards me. I noticed his attractive hand, slender and groomed.

He wore an immaculately white Afghan Peraan Tombaan ["Shirt & Pants"], with a dark-blue vest, the top button of the shirt undone. To me he looked very handsome in it. He was reasonably tall – with my four-centimetre heels he was a bit

---

[8] Headscarf; not be confused with "chadori" the body-engulfing, mostly blue, garment

taller than me, so I estimated him to be between one seventy-five and one-eighty. He was smaller in overall size than one might have imagined. Yet he commanded a strong presence due to his appearance.

He was slim, his wavy hair all neatly tucked away under his trademark pakul, which he mostly wore slightly slanted to the back of his head.

"He was a tall man, but not physically imposing. He was quiet and formal, yet he radiated intensity", observed Steve Coll in his book "Ghost Wars".

And this was true. Subtle qualities which left me spell-bound from the start!

Not knowing at first which language to address me in he inquired with J.B. Once he found out that he could speak in French he turned to me and said:

"Mademoiselle, it is nice to meet you. Welcome to Afghanistan!

He looked at me with his intense eyes. Eyes so unparalleled, that they are hard to describe. They fixated you with their calm depth and quick intelligence. To me they have stayed the most beautiful eyes I have ever seen.

"Thank you, Sir," I replied with a smile, trying to control my trembling hands by folding them in front of my body. "Thank you for allowing me to come here".

"It is my pleasure. - Your French is very good."

"Thank you – yours, too." I replied, looking straight at him, smiling.

For the first time I was slotting in a little joke, quite aware of the slightly inappropriate undertone to that sentence. Who was I to compliment him? But he caught on with it immediately and laughed.

"Thank you. - Come, let's have dinner." He finally said in his calm manly voice.

He then turned around to re-join his men, not before showing us the way, me walking in front of him. He then boarded his car and left us to follow in our own vehicle.

In September 2005 I was introduced to Ahmad Massoud, his son, at the occasion of his father's 4th death anniversary. 16 years old then and an intelligent boy, he knew immediately who I was, proofing to me yet again that my relationship with his father had been an open secret. He tried hard to look like his father. While he wore the pakul of course and resembles him, his face is still different and his eyes do not exude the same striking fire.

That afternoon he brought me to the family's house in Jangalak. While we settled down for tea he said:

"I am very glad we finally meet. I remember you being around a lot, but since you never came to our house, I never met you. When I once asked mother 'who is this foreign woman?' she simply said, 'she is helping father'". He paused, while I smiled into my teacup then raised my head.

"I am happy, too. I met with your mother after your father's death. She was too friendly for the fact that ... you know. But I was glad."

"I have been wanting to show you this" the boy continued and took out a notebook from his bag. It was one of his father's diaries.

"I have been reading them one by one" he said in a quiet voice "and when I read about you, I wanted to meet you."

"I am in there?" I asked rather stupidly.

"Yes of course. I thought perhaps you might like to know a little about what my father has written about you"

"Oh yes, yes of course ..." I said in a confused manner

The boy opened the notebook:

"This is what he wrote on the day you were first introduced."

27 Shahrivar 1376 (18th Sept 1997)

Today J.B. visited yet again. He and the television crew he brought along have been here for two days already. Once again, I had to make him wait.

What a joy it is always to meet old friends. They open your heart – they let you breath the free air of friendship. No strife – just joy.

This time he brought along a woman.

Some people capture you from the minute you lay eyes on them. I should not be writing this – may Allah forgive me – but Ariana has touched me somewhere deep inside. An excitement has besieged me – she is physically attractive, but there is something else. I have only just met her, yet I feel a connection I cannot describe – may Allah forgive me!'

"My father loved you deeply.

I must tell you, Madar ["mother" – used to address older women by young people, regardless of relationship], I was first upset that he loved anyone else but my mother. But

34

then, reading his diary, I came to understand what he felt, what you felt for each other. I hope one day Allah will grant me a woman like you."

I was stunned to hear the young man talk in such a manner. At the same time, I had tears well up in my eyes from the words I had just read. So, it was all true – he had fallen for me the day we met, just like I had fallen for him the day I saw him years before he saw me.

I stroked Ahmad's cheek then took him into my arms, tears running down my face.

"Thank you, Bach-im [my boy], for sharing this with me".

Ever since this introduction I have divided my life into before and after meeting Massoud. People who do not know him will think this to be exaggerated, many of those who do will understand me.

As we were walking towards the cars which would bring us to Jangalak, the all-observant J.B. gave me a cheeky smile "you like him, non?"

"J.B., 'like' is a huge understatement" I replied, "I am totally flat out".

"You must be careful, though," he said after a moment while the smile ran away from his face "you cannot show this in any way. People are shy here and women are expected to be reserved."

"Of course! – I would never think of it!" I protested, embarrassed that I obviously wore my heart on my sleeve for everyone to spot.

Wherever we walked, whatever we did that evening, my eyes were pealed on Massoud. He was more attractive than any photograph could have communicated. His eyes, his smile, his voice and speech, his entire appearance and demeanour just overwhelmed me. Not everybody would have agreed to say that he was handsome. Some would have described his face to be on the haggard side, with lines carving the corners of his eyes whenever he smiled and his cheeks appearing hollow at times.

He had the most varied face – later I would learn that his feelings were displayed there for everyone to see if one was only able to read.

From one second to the other his expression would change from a relaxed one to a serious one.

But whichever expression he offered, to me he was the most attractive man I had ever come across.

He had this incredible force to his face, which spoke of a determined character, forceful in a positive way, never communicating fear, just determination. His gestures spoke the same language - one could see that he was a natural leader and powerful figure. Yet he never suggested domination over others, people just naturally followed him. It was amazing to see.

And his eyes, oh his eyes – they would look straight at you into your heart. Those with an inferior nature could often not stand his gaze. Me, I was mesmerised by them, they swept me away, down those dark irises into a place far away from war and suffering into a realm of beauty and peace.

He was neat in everything he did. The way he dressed, the way he gestured - everything was to the point, clean and clear. He asked precise questions. If the answer did not contain enough detail, he would re-iterate. That fact was one of the reasons why we would get on so well later.

Massoud's house was a simple L-shaped one-storey building with the typical large Afghan window frames. Built from brown mud bricks, all these houses blended into the landscape of rocks, green treelines, mountains, the river, and dust-devils.

The Panjshir is often windy and that day it was no different. The trees outside the windows moved in the blue sky. As we settled down the sun had almost set and the wind slowly subsided.

As we sat down in local style on floor cushions for dinner in his house, there were no commanders that night, just our crew, J.B., myself, Dr. Abdullah and Massoud Khallili, the Northern Alliance ambassador to India.

Right after dinner our crew left. I sat next to J.B., opposite Massoud, his close presence wrapping me in a warm excitement.

An aide brought tea.

The soft light of the two gas lamps in two corners of the room created a warm atmosphere and added to my feeling of total comfort.

More relaxed now, Massoud turned to J.B. and asked him in Dari whether I minded if he asked me a few questions. J.B. translated, and I replied:

"No, of course not Sir, what would you like to know?"

Continuing in French he began:

"You are German, right? But you live in Singapore?"

"Yes, that's right. I have been living in Asia for a long time, so I consider it my cultural home." I smiled at him, then looked away.

"What do you like about Asia?"

"Many things, Sir. I love particularly India, Persia, and everything in between. Those are just such rich cultures, genuine. The people on average are spirited and complex – I love that. Despite all problems."

"What made you come to Afghanistan?"

I panicked. What was I to say? I could not possibly tell him the truth!

After a quick help-beckoning look at J.B., which did not yield any result, I found the escape:

"The Afghan Tragedy, Sir. I have suffered with your country for many years and her continued peril strikes my heart at the core. I wanted to see with my own eyes this country you have been fighting for for almost two decades now."

"So now that you are here, what do you think?"

"It is most beautiful, and I am beginning to understand why you love your country, why you are fighting to preserve the Afghan way of life."

He nodded.

"I hear Singapore is a real spectacular example of successful and efficient development – is that true?"

"Well, it is. The government institutions work well, there is virtually no corruption and the government – even though rather tightly controlling – has done an excellent job in modernising and developing the country. And most of all they managed to integrate the various ethnic groups and their religions which live there. Chinese, Indians and Malays.

But as you might imagine there is always a flipside to every coin: everything is quite tightly controlled; personal, and democratic expression is limited, stifling creativity.

Personally, I am having problems with people's attitudes there – I don't want to get into details as one can only understand when one has lived there for a while – but I prefer countries with rougher edges than Singapore. But of course, then again there are far worse places to live in."

"Interesting ... Do you think you could organise me some books on the Singapore development, the government etc.?"

"Oh yes, definitely. I can send some to you. They would have to be in English, maybe in French, though, as we do not have Persian literature in Singapore."

"I would much appreciate that."

He looked at me for a long second. Me, too insecure yet to stand his gaze, I lowered my eyes.

Other than that, I had to control myself not to be found looking at him all the time. I tried to lower my head frequently, giving my gaze a rest. Only when he spoke, I allowed myself to look at him all the way. What a fascinating person!

The seeds of extreme attraction started to break through the soil of my heart right here – here, that evening. They had been sown many years ago when I started to learn about him. But now the warm rain of his presence, demeanour and personality made them come to life.

Swept away – drop by drop

15th October 1997

We had been here for almost a month and our adventure was about to come to an end.

With every day my mood had become more dampened, corresponding with the colder weather that had set in. Day by day it became clearer to me that it was going to be the hardest thing for me to leave Massoud.

During these few weeks we had spent a lot of time with him and had shared many personal moments, had followed a major offensive against the Taliban who attempted to take the Panjshir Valley. We had experienced every detail of his operational set-up – all of which will be edged into my memory until the day I die.

We followed in detail how he and his commanders prepared for attacks and other operations. How they sometimes spent nights without sleep pouring over maps to figure out the best strategy. We had the chance to meet several Massoud's fellow decision makers and advisors, most of whom, after his death exercised and still exercise influence of varying degrees in the political arena in Kabul.

We had seen success and failure, triumph, and death. We experienced emotional ups and downs; the terror brought about by war inevitably. But this story is not mainly about these things. They have been well documented before.

Mostly Massoud would be occupied with his commanders and would be engaged in various civilian projects personally. Often, he would not pay much attention to us and the crew but had given permission for us to follow him everywhere, nothing was off-limits, except for his family, his private sphere.

There were, however, quiet moments where he was there for us alone, when he would engage with us, answer J.B.'s questions, simply have a conversation with us. And then of course there were the dinners we took, the times we sat down to have tea with him – alone or with his other men.

Whenever I had the chance to speak to Massoud directly my pulse started racing and despite J.B.'s advice I could not resist to engage with him just this little bit. I would always look him straight into his beautiful intense eyes, sometimes covering the rest of my faces with my scarf. I was so insecure still, my voice trembling at times. But I tried to cover it up with a smile each time.

One day we followed him by helicopter to an area close to the Tajik border – the town of Taloqan where he had established his local base outside of the Panjshir. In early 1998, when the Taliban had managed to encircle his territory, he relocated his headquarters there but was again forced to relocate further north in September 2000 to the district of Khwaja Bahaudin. The Panjshir, however, could always be defended against the Taliban after a major advance against the valley had been fended off in July 1997.

"See" he said approaching me from behind as we were standing on a hilltop on a chilly clear morning, "over there is Tajikistan. Close, isn't it?" He pulled his black and white scarf, which was wrapped around his neck over his nose to protect him from the cold air.

"And just a few miles that way is Taliban territory. Last night it took our men hours to re-take just one single but strategically important hill. So, we pushed them back at least a little bit."

I looked out over the rolling hills below and signalled my understanding. The scenery was all covered in thin blue mist. It was an amazing view and despite the continued tragedy which brought us here I felt very happy and excited. It was cold but while I spoke to Massoud - despite my nerves - I felt so comfortable, I simply enjoyed every word we exchanged. Everything flowed, even though we had only known each other for a short while.

He had no reason to talk to me directly; there was no reason to explain anything to me. So, since he did so anyway, I gathered that he enjoyed my company and seemed to seek it. Or was he just being polite? Was this just a figment of my imagination?

I never approached him myself. But when he approached me, I gave him my full attention and hoped to make it clear that I enjoyed his company. I told myself repeatedly that he was just being polite. Anyway, we all knew that we were going to leave again soon.

On days during which Massoud was kept away from us we had time for "excursions" into the Northern Alliance territory where we found laid bare the terrible state the country had slipped into after nearly twenty years of conflict. We found refugee camps with hundreds of people cramped into limited numbers of makeshift tents. Draught had worsened the situation over the last year bringing food supplies to a minimum. Still people were fleeing the Taliban controlled areas into the Northern Alliance controlled ones to escape the harsh Islamic rule established by the first.

We had plenty of time to explore the Panjshir Valley – the Shir-e-Panjshir's [Lion of Panjshir] home base. He was beginning to make a big difference in this part of Afghanistan – on the political level by establishing local shuras [councils] for villagers to decide on their own affairs, as well as on the civilian level. Massoud made it a point to be involved in most every civilian construction effort in the Panjshir. Here he was not only army general but also head of the local decision bodies.

As in the Panjshir, Massoud built up a political and administrative infrastructure under the SCN (Supervisory Council of the North, consisting of various Jamiat commanders thereby covering various northern provinces) umbrella, too. The SCN included sub-councils consisting of commanders, religious leaders, and village elders. There were six functional committees in addition to the military committee that planned and conducted armed operations. They dealt with finance, health, education and culture, political affairs, and information. Each of the sub-committees employed hundreds of people. With Massoud's ability to draw people towards him he managed to recruit skilled and motivated individuals especially from among Panjshiris with professional experience in Kabul.

He used his superior organisational skill to build up village militias and mujahedin bases (one for every six or seven villages), which could be used to stage defensive and offensive operations. There were 20 such bases in the Panjshir Valley. Massoud also organised a more mobile striking force under his personal command. It was composed of young volunteers who were required to be literate, were highly trained and wore uniforms. In the war against the Soviets Massoud had used these commandos to ambush Soviet supply convoys.

Already in 1985 Massoud had convened a shura of Jamiat commanders from five north-eastern provinces to coordinate their activities, reorganise and train their forces and contribute volunteers to the formation of central fighting units und his direct control. As before, they were composed of literate volunteers who trained and fought together without regard to local origin or party and used Dari as their language of command. As Massoud's reputation as the "Lion of Panjshir" spread nationally, more young Afghan volunteers, particularly from non-Pashtun areas flocked to his standard.

When he had time for us, especially during and after dinners, we had lengthy conversations on many things. He was extremely curious on all aspects of my life and wanted to know what places I had been, why I left Europe, what was Europe like, what was Southeast Asia like and many more. Each time I thoroughly enjoyed every second of it and if I was in love with him when I met him, I was even more in love after this month for all that he was. I still did not take these conversations as any personal interest. I had heard and read before that he liked to learn from all foreigners he met as much as he could about their cultures and countries.

"What have you been doing in Singapore all these years?" was one of his questions.

"I have essentially run a business with a partner in the logistics area. It is a household removal business. There is quite a lucrative market in Singapore as there are many expatriate families living and working there for several years. And when they come and go, they need removal services for their household goods."

"I see. That is interesting. How did you think of getting into this line?"

"Before going to Singapore I lived in China for 3 years. There I already worked for an international household removal company and gained all the expertise to run one myself. But I needed funding – so this is how I pulled in my partner."

"That seems to be a service which is popular in developed countries. First of all, the phenomenon of moving to another place and then bringing all your things with you. See, in Afghanistan most people will live in the place they were born in for most of their life. It's only the women who move to their husband's house after their wedding. – In my case, though, it was different" he laughed "I had to move in with my wife due to circumstances and had to bring my parents along, too". He was referring to the fact that during the Soviet occupation his parents' house in the Panjshir had been squatted by soldiers and subsequently turned into an orphanage. After the occupiers left, Massoud left the house as an orphanage and brought his parents to live with his wife's family until his father's death in a car accident in 1992.

"I remember my brother Wali telling me some years ago that he needed to move house in London. That was a grand affair – it appeared to me – as he involved all sorts of people to accomplish the move. Afterwards he told me that he should have engaged a removal company to do the job for him."

He laughed again. His laugh was infectious, his face, the joy springing from it, made me smile myself – he laughed from the bottom of his heart, careless and joyful.

It had noticed after a while that we were two birds of a feather. We thought alike in so many areas of politics, philosophy, faith, had many similar likes and dislikes. We found ourselves rather often in the situation where either

45

one of us said "I was just thinking the same thing" or "I was just about to say that".

He actively involved me in all these conversations, even when talking to someone else in our group. He looked at me frequently and seemed to enjoy it when I challenged him on something.

One thorny issue which came up once was the Northern Alliance attempt to repel the Taliban forces out of Kabul just this past July for another try at power. I put it to him that perhaps it had not been wise to attempt that, as the results had shown. Should there not have been a longer preparation period?

"I was asked this same question before the offensive by another journalist, who accompanied us then. He even wrote me a long letter on it." he set out. "You know, you make decisions at your best ability at the time – it's always like that. And this seemed like a good time slot for an offensive. As it turned out – but one never knows that in advance – we could not re-take Kabul. Now we are in the defensive and we won't get a chance soon to take over Kabul again, but it was worth a try – I still maintain that. The problem is that the support for the Talibs is too strong." He paused. The lines crossing his forehead suddenly deepened. I nodded in understanding.

It was in these conversations that I discovered his convictions and vision for the future of Afghanistan and her society.

Mostly, however, it was the actions he took for the people under his control, which demonstrated without many words what he believed in. The continued suffering of the Afghan people seemed to torment him and it was with his heart and soul that he wished for a stable and peaceful yet strong and independent country.

All accusations of him fighting for fighting sake are utter nonsense and whoever has and will bring up such statements has not even scratched the surface of this man's mind. Whatever connotations people have with "war-lords" he certainly did not fit that bill. J.B. once put it to a journalist as follows:

"Massoud was a friend, he was more than a military man — he was a man of culture. We would sit for hours at night reciting poetry. When I talked to Massoud, I realized that I had in front of me, a man of history, not just of Afghanistan."

About his vision for the country he said:.

"I see a free Afghanistan, independent. A country where her people elect a council of elders, a Loya Jirga, composed out of hundreds of representatives. A country where the government is elected, and the arms are surrendered. I see the Mujahedin put together an army of reconstruction and an army of education. I see girls go to school just like boys. I see a traditional agricultural system, interwoven with our ancestral land. I see our historic and cultural heritage preserved and valued as this is our memory. Finally, I see all children of Abraham live in peace in our world."

He continued with a thoughtful and candid look in his eyes:

"I have started to create this in the Panjshir. I hope that one day I can contribute to putting in place an Afghan assembly of such nature. And perhaps the world could be interested in a model like that. "

J.B. challenged him then:

"But democracies already exist in the West, with the principle of assemblies."

But he replied:

"No, these are not real democracies. A democracy does not tolerate the Taliban, people so far removed from one's own principles, only out of economic interests. We need to, once more, envision and apply a real democracy."

So simple, yet so touching, these words have stuck in my memory because he could not drive them home to the relevant governments. He could not convince them of his benevolent intentions. Instead, he fell victim to international circumstances, political decisions and internally to the lack of responsible partners in his fight for his ideals. In retrospect these words cut me deeply because this failure resulted in his continued struggle which he did not survive.

"What do you think of democracy?" he turned to me then.

"Well, there is no easy answer to that question" I began. "But first I would like to say that I could not agree more with what you just said. Your vision is very beautiful, and I hope that you will be able to make it a reality."

"Thank you." He smiled.

"Parliamentary democracy is not a perfect system of governance. Anyway, there is no such thing. We should be aware that it is the smallest evil and hence should be the choice for every country regardless of its flaws. But and that is important, the democratic system installed should pay respect to the situation in the country both societal and cultural. There is no one size fits all. In the case of Afghanistan, for example, the system installed must cater to integrating the country above all rather than – in an attempt to give every little group a voice – further fragmenting the country. Yet it will be important to give the larger ethnic groups adequate representation. At the same time, it needs to be ensured that no regional power holders are allowed to undermine the unity of the country."

"I fully agree" Massoud nodded "the system installed needs to pay respect to the different aspects of Afghanistan. And these are complicated indeed. We all know how much tribal frictions have contributed to the situation we have now. I myself am not free of blame in this regard. When we took Kabul and took power the various Mujahedin parties should have been more united. But that is a different topic altogether.

You know, I have never been able to forgive the Americans that they have stopped supporting our cause after the Soviet Union withdrew. They say that they are the vanguards of democracy and human rights in the world but now they are about to support and recognise those who are spitting on those values. Then again, on the other hand, they have now re-approached us with the singular purpose of capturing Osama Bin Laden. What they still not care about is the overall plight Afghanistan has been enduring. Such political tactics show that a country always must guard its independence. If not, she will be reduced to an extra in other people's play." His face turned very serious.

"True" I nodded, "one should be especially careful with the Americans. They have certain interests in this and other parts of the world and that's that. Afghanistan will be the stepping-stone into Central Asia for them, to all its oil reserves. That is why they do not care which regime can provide stability here – a democratically elected one or the Talilban.

We must remember this: The Clinton administration supports an oil and gas pipeline from Turkmenistan through Afghanistan to Gwadar. Unocal is seeking the rights to build this pipeline, and have entered into negotiations with the Taliban, to secure protection for the pipeline. So, there we see that they have no scruples."

"Yes, you are well informed. The oil – that is another point." he added.

"And I believe you have met on several occasions with Robin Rafael, am I right? - She's a hawk if it comes to these things. You know this better than me."

Robin Rafael, the Assistant Secretary of State for Central Asian Affairs, stationed in Pakistan at the time had had the cheek to suggest in her last meeting with Massoud earlier that year, that his best option would be to surrender to the Taliban, prompting him to throw his Pakul onto the table, stating that as long as he controlled a chunk of the country the size of his hat, he'd never surrender.

"Oh yes, she is. Our recent meeting didn't go very well and I believe it was our last one. Something tells me that you know what happened." He smiled at me.

"Yes, Sir. I will just say 'pakul'", I smirked.

He laughed. "Yes".

"Striking a deal with the Americans might mean opening Pandora's box of dependence. They have not cared of the intricate workings of tribal feuding here and I bet you that 90% of Congress has not heard your name or the values you stand for. You see, the average Westerner has no clue of what your struggle means. They do not have the religious or other passion necessary to fight any such war. The West has lost many values, which would enable them to understand. To most of the European and American public Afghanistan is just another country where chaos reigns. Few people value your culture, even fewer value Islam. So public opinion so far does not work in your favour there.

But if I may say something?"

"Yes of course please speak your mind ..."

"You, Amir Sahib, would have the power to influence public opinion in the West, if only properly propagated. I am very convinced about that."

"Why do you say that?"

"Again, this is my very personal opinion; please forgive me for speaking too upfront."

"No, no please, please continue. I am interested in what you have to say."

"You bring along the charisma to convince people of your cause. You will be able to engage them with your personality. The media is a very powerful weapon in the West, often called the "forth power" next to the traditional three of democratic institutions: legislature, judiciary, and law-enforcement. Of course, some time and money would have to be spent but I think it's about high tide to give the SCN the profile you all deserve. The American stance is simply unacceptable, and it will end in a disaster one day, at least for the Afghan people. That's all I should say right now."

I smiled at him then looked down into my teacup. What I actually meant to say was that he had the attraction and human touch, the honesty and benevolence, which would influence people, touch them, like he already had touched many in his own country and abroad, like he had touched me. But I could not say that. Not here. Not now.

"Right ..." he said, giving me a long thoughtful look which I reciprocated this time. I had talked to him so much during this last month that I had gotten very comfortable under his gaze.

Massoud was also a devout Muslim. He prayed – wherever possible – five times a day. He read the Koran most every night. He did not follow just the form but was a deeply religious man. Not only did he lead his men in battle but also in prayer.

Most every meeting with his commanders would start with a few words from the Koran or a brief prayer.

He was, however, never an extremist "neither in his political nor private life" as his brother Wali once put it. "His practise of Islam was as soft as the Panjshir peach." A most beautiful analogy, I found.

God loving, he had a deep sense of spirituality and appreciated all religions' paths to God. He felt that faith was a very private matter and not to be forced upon others. In his vision for the country there was space for all religions, even though Islam was to be the general religion of the country. He would have never favoured a secular society, as he believed that Afghanistan had to be rooted in a moderate Islam. This had formed the basis why he – as a very young man - had joined the fight against the Soviets. He had become more of a nationalist ever since, arguing for religion's limited influence on politics, but this basic conviction has always remained the same.

Among others we found common ground in our appreciation of the Sufis' "mysticism". We talked at length about the connection and similarities between Indian religions and Sufism such as the experience of God through a state of ecstasy. That means agreeing on the fact that God can be experienced in this world rather than waiting for a God-experience after death.

I cited the Sikh believe system as an example, the concept of a Guru as the messenger and personal guardian on our path to God.

"Just what is the Prophet to you, this is what the Guru is to the Sikhs. Also, many Hindus have a guru: a holy man who shows them the path to God."

When it came to religious topics, we left the rest of the crew and even J.B. behind very fast. After a few minutes it was him and me talking alone. We never argued, we just talked, as we agreed on all these things.

"How often have you been to India?" Massoud Khalili asked me during our first dinner.

"Many times, Sir."

"Where did you go?"

"Mainly places in the north. From Panjab all the way to Varanasi and West Bengal."

"Would you go and pray in a Hindu temple?" Massoud asked.

"Yes, I would"

"But both our religions teach that there is only one God — how do you deal with Hinduism's many Gods?"

"I believe that all religions teach the same — the truth is only buried in misinterpretations of the Holy Scriptures and differences come in because different elements of that same truth are being stressed. Hinduism, for example, celebrates the fact that the one God — Brahma — is present in all of creation; hence they have created the millions of Gods for the ordinary worshipper to understand this fact. But in reality, there is only one. We should in fact worship God in each element of creation because He is all of that. Without His creativity none of this could exist, it all would disappear. Hinduism and Sikhism believe that this entire world is a dream, created each second by God. Once he stops dreaming, this world will just vanish. As such God is the only real existence, the only truth.

To me every temple, mosque etc is a house of prayer and holy."

Massoud had followed each of my words with inspired attention.

"Very interesting" he looked at me. "Tell me more."

"What would you like to know?"

"What do Sikhs, for example, believe is the after-life like?"

"Well, they believe that, after we leave our body, we enter a world far more beautiful than this, where there is no pain, no worries, no hunger. All the ailments of this world are absent. But for the moment that abode is only temporary as we will have to return to this plain in another body. We re-incarnate many more times until our karma – both positive and negative, by the way - is worked out and we deserve to stay on the other plain. There more karma is to be removed until we reach final liberation in God as a free soul, no more bound to a body of whichever matter. This liberation – which the Buddhists call Nirvana – means endless, always new happiness, never-ending love and joy in God."

"It is very rare to see a Westerner speak of Eastern believes in such a fashion. Usually, I find most Westerners are not religious. That is one reason why I believe that Western society models cannot simply be transplanted into Afghanistan. Many people here are deeply religious with many impacts on societal conditions. And those are good, not to be thrown away."

"And I agree with you, Sir. Western societies have gone down a wrong path in this respect."

"Yes, I can see that you think very oriental – very interesting." He smiled at me. "I would like to talk more to you about this, but I think we are boring everybody else," he looked around with a cheeky smile "especially J.B." he mocked his friend.

"I am just more of a reality-based person" J.B. tried to justify himself.

"One day I would like to talk to you more about faith. It is very interesting, and you have a beautiful attitude." He smiled at me and finally wrapped this topic up.

"I would love that." I said, then lowered my eyes. I did not assume at that point that we would ever get around to that. But this compliment he gave me made me fly. It was the first time that he had taken this much personal interest in me.

Finally, and most memorably, there was an evening spent by our crew, J.B., Massoud, Massoud Khalili and me in the Northern Alliance Guesthouse in the Panjshir four days before we were scheduled to leave Afghanistan. You could say it was a farewell get-together.

After we had taken dinner, we all gathered in the lounge sitting down on the sofas. The caretaker served us tea and the men started talking among themselves. I sat in an armchair near the window, sipping my tea, and observing Massoud. He gave such serious attention to the people he spoke to. He spoke quietly and respectfully.

After a while his eyes wandered across the room and when he saw me sitting by the window he said:

"Ariana, I sometimes see you walking around with those headphones plugged into your ears ... what device is that?"

"Oh, you must be talking about my "disc man". It's a portable CD player. It's a fairly new gadget from Japan." I explained, turning to J.B. for help in translating 'disc man'.

"I see. What music are you listening to?"

"Indian music, mainly" I replied.

"Do you mind, can I listen to some?"

"Yes, of course. In fact, I brought two small speakers along, which can be connected to the player. Then everybody can listen to it."

I went to my room to get the player and the pocket-sized speakers and after I had set it all up, I started playing the songs.

The CD I picked had a random mix on it – fast songs followed love songs and so forth.

So, after a few tracks, with one famous Hindi love song starting, I turned to Khalili, and asked him "Ambassador, you must know this one ... ?"

Khalili turned his head, listen for a second and said, "Oh yes, of course! I loved that movie!" And then, to everybody's surprise, a few seconds into the song he got up and started singing the male part of the duet and signalled me to sing the female part.

"Wah-wah-wah!" I exclaimed, clapping my hands, at first refusing to get up, just clapping along.

The song – most fittingly – was called "when I looked at you, I learned this, darling (that love is crazy).[9]"

But Khalili insisted, so I got up reluctantly and started moving with the music while at the same time trying to remember the words. I felt exposed. I had Massoud's eyes on me.

I focused on Khalili as my duet partner to resist the temptation to look back at him.

When we were finished everybody started clapping and laughing, one of the camera men even whistled with his fingers. Khalili came up to me and pretended to circle money

---

[9] तुझे देखा तो यह जाना सनम (tujhe deka to ye jana sanam) from the movie "The courageous will take the bride"

around my head, a common gesture in India when a performer pleases the audience, but then of course it is actual money. I threw my head back in embarrassment, burying my face in my hands and sat back down. To focus my attention, I grabbed my teacup and emptied it in one gulp.

After a couple of more tracks a Qawali song by Nusrat Fateh Ali Khan – a famous Pakistani Sufi singer – came on.

I turned to Massoud:

"You must like Qawali, Sir, am I right?"

"Oh yes, very much. I just did not have the chance to listen to any for years."

"Do you know Nusrat Fateh Ali Khan?"

"Yes, I have heard of him. He is Pakistani, isn't he?"

"Yes, but he sings mainly in Panjabi, not Urdu. Like this song – it's also in Panjabi. Do you understand anything?"

"No, not really. It's still quite different from Urdu, right?"

"Yes, quite – I also only understand very little. But I know what this song means …"

"Oh yes, what?"

"It's called "Biba sada dil more de" The refrain goes: 'if you can't stay in front of my eyes, leave my heart, too.'" I translated into French.

"I find these two simple lines communicate so much sadness. Impossible love is one of the most terrible things that can happen." I smiled at him.

"Do you think so?"

"Yes – if the person you have fallen for does not reciprocate your love, for which ever reason, it tears your heart apart to such a degree that all joy of life disappears."

"Hm" he nodded, smiling, then quickly looked away.

After we had all dispersed that evening J.B. approached me as I was standing outside on the guesthouse's terrace taking in the cool night air before retiring to my room:

"You have cast a spell on him, do you realise that?" He said in a half joking half serious manner.

"How do you mean?"

"How do I mean?" J.B raised his eyebrows. "He watched you all the while. And there are not many women here who are moving this skilfully in front of men either. So, yah, I should say that you caught his attention" he added sarcastically. It was the first time I saw him really not pleased.

I wrapped myself more tightly in my coat and took a deep breath of the star-filled air, looking up into the sky.

"But come on! It was all Khalili's fault" I tried to appease him with a quip. "He practically forced me".

"Yes, right! And that armchair you were sitting in looked very uncomfortable, too." He couldn't resist grinning at his own sarcasm.

That night sleep evaded me until three or four in the morning. I was too excited, too wrapped up in my emotions. The desire to be loved by him overcame me like never before. The feeling that I would die inside if he broke my heart became overpowering that night.

Point of no return

After all of this I found it impossible to conceive that in three days' time all this should be history – a one off never to be repeated? I should never see Massoud again? My heart did not leave any room for that, there was just no way. Before I even left, I felt a sense of emptiness and longing.

But what was I going to do? And even if I devised another plan, would he ever reciprocate my feelings, much less act on them? If not, then what? Would everything end in silent heartbreak and despair, one day waking up to the realisation of how stupid I had been?

Despite J.B.'s nervous reaction to yesterday's events, the next morning, I decided to push it even further as for the third time a plan was hatching in my mind – in this case a plan I was not sure of. Could I cope with it or not? Was it a good idea in the first place or just a product of my emotions gone wild? Yet I felt I was in an all or nothing situation. So, I approached J.B. after dinner with a trembling heart while he was sitting outside on the big veranda of our guesthouse watching the sun set.

"J.B." I began "how do you feel I have done out here? Did you regret at any point having brought me along?"

"Oh, I thought you were great. You coped with all situations very well. The fact that Massoud let you go down to the front line with us the other day shows that he has full confidence in you to know how to conduct yourself. So, who am I to say otherwise?" he smiled.

"Thank you, I appreciate that. In fact, I was really surprised that I was allowed to join you guys as a woman down at the front. I will never forget that experience. I had never even heard a shot fired before I came here and then I had shells fly over my head and rocket launchers going off next to me."

We just sat quietly after that for several minutes looking out over the mountains and the river flowing below. The mountain peaks were painted in gold by the setting sun, while the valley below was already covered in shadows. This being October it was already fairly chilli at that time of day.

"Do you think Massoud could need some help at any end?" I finally said into the silence, turning to J.B. while moving some stubborn hair out of my face which the wind kept dragging out from below my headscarf.

"How do you mean?"

"Well, does he need any non-military help to support his cause?"

"I am sure he will take any help he can get his hands on – do you want to donate money?"

"Not really. I think all my savings will not get this endeavour far." I laughed, "I was more thinking of getting involved myself"

For the second time since we met, I saw J.B. look at me in disbelieve and seemed to worry about my level of sanity.

"I'm reminding you that I said not to push it. I'm getting worried here. But regardless: What do have in mind?" He asked with his forehead in frowns.

"J.B., you know how I feel about Massoud and his cause. Do you think that you could talk to him about any suitable back-up function, a secretary position, whatever, where I could bring in my language abilities and office experience to help boost his cause; perhaps for the international or media relations side of things – I don't know; something along those lines. You see, I really don't know whether what I am asking makes any sense, but this is what my heart is asking me to do."

Again, I must have looked at him with great desperation as he agreed to talk to Massoud. But this time he said:

"Don't keep your hopes anywhere near high. Because that is something else you are requesting here. Are you sure that is what you want me to ask him? You know, you should not be doing this in the hope that he will start an affair with you. You will be totally heart broken. He has a wife he loves and children he adores. If you really want to make a difference here, I will ask him, if it's for the former I'd rather not."

"J.B., I won't lie to you. It is for both reasons. I do very badly want to make a difference here. At the same time what I feel for Massoud is beyond compare. But I promise you across my heart that no initiative will come from me. If he disappoints me – so be it. But I must give it a try. My hopes are already sky-high; I can't help it. So please do me this momentous favour. If he agrees I will be in your dept for the rest of my life.

Maybe you can remind him of what he said some two weeks ago, when he spoke of his vision for Afghanistan. Tell him that I want to help him realise this vision because I share it from the bottom of my heart."

18th October 1997

It was the day before our intended departure.

When I got up, I saw the helicopter take off from our side of the river. An unmistakable sign that Massoud was leaving the valley. At that moment J.B. knocked on my door and walked in with the broadest smile on his face.

"Where is Amir Sahib going?" I asked without wishing him a good morning.

"Up to Taloqan. And good morning to you, too" came the reply. "But he will be back again tomorrow to help you settle in after I have left."

I was packing some things into my bag mumbling "sorry, good morning" and was deep in thought of what could have possibly happened to my request. Why was he taking off without saying good-bye, what was going on? Was all this again one of my illusions, built up in my mind? A colourful bubble about to burst. Yes, of course, he probably had laughed at this silly and revealing idea and had told J.B. to take me back. Yes, silly it was, driven by emotions, a Scorpio's misdirected willpower. What was a woman to do here? A woman who did not speak a word of the language? What could she possibly contribute?

It took J.B.'s last sentence about a minute to reach my brain ...."What?"

"Yes, I spoke to him early this morning over breakfast. He was hesitant at first as he is worried about your safety and how you are going to settle in, not to mention the way this might be viewed by his men. But eventually he agreed, and he has already a whole list of ideas on how you can help him. Overall, you will be happy to hear that he was positively surprised.

He is thinking of letting you work together with Abdullah on the international relations aspects and give you several civilian projects to work on. He also wants to capitalise on your political system insights and help him conceptualise the political future of Afghanistan. Of course, though, you will have to learn Dari and that quite fast.

He feels he needs to raise the Northern Alliances political profile above and beyond the "mujahedin" image. He won't be able to pay you, but your livelihood will be well taken care of. And of course, if this whole endeavour succeeds you, like every leading figure of the Northern Alliance, will be rewarded for your hard work and endurance. Here, this guesthouse is yours to stay in permanently whenever you are in the Panjshir, all food and everything else will be taken care of. Between the two of us: you won't miss a thing. Massoud will see to that. Trust me.

As you know – the Taliban have covered a lot of ground lately and Massoud wants to concentrate the resistance on the northwest front. That's why you all will be re-located to Taloqan near the Tajik boarder where he intends to establish his local headquarters."

Again, I found myself gasping for air. This was not real, was it?

The following day J.B. and the film crew left Afghanistan as planned.

Below the rotating helicopter blades, I was close to tears.

"Thank you so very much for what you have done for me. I don't know how to ever thank you. I am forever in your debt. Take care now and write to me whenever you can. Once this documentary is ready, please send me a copy."

"I will. You take care now. Be very careful in whatever you do. This is still a war zone. This is still a country you do not know well.

Bring Massoud to Europe. It would be good for him to gain political profile there. And when you do, we will meet again."

With that he boarded the helicopter and, holding my headscarf down from the surging wind, I watched them disappear.

Two days later I received a call from J.B. telling me that he was safely back in Paris and the crew had already made their way back to New York.

"Even a journey of a thousand miles begins with one single step"
(Chinese proverb)

Since his decision that I could stay I joined Massoud and Abdullah in the Panjshir from November 1997 for the purpose of getting involved with several of the civilian projects the Lion of Panjshir had launched there. - Schools for all children, not only boys, bridges, clean water supplies, hospitals and many more endeavours were on the way.

Prior to that I flew back to Singapore by way of Dushanbe to move out of my apartment and pack a few useful things, such as medicine, clothes, and hygiene products. I also managed to organise several books on the Singaporean political and economic system which I had promised to Massoud. My excess luggage was 60kg.

Soon the whole valley knew about me.

I was mainly involved in projects related to women, such as schools for girls, and hospital-related projects where I dealt with nurses and female doctors, some of them had returned to the war-torn country of their birth from overseas. In such a secretive world of the women it was easy to find real friends. Most Afghans are hospitable, but from woman-to-woman great bonds developed. I was lucky enough to gain the trust of many and, despite my initial language impediment, managed to put the direction into the projects which Massoud wanted to see.

This work was important for me, not only to familiarise myself with everything and get down and dirty, but also for me to draw a full picture of what Massoud and his men had been doing in the territories they controlled other than military action. It was important to highlight his political efforts of grassroots democracy, the shuras he had organised etc; it was important in order to convey his wide-reaching vision for the country, rather than leaving the field open to his enemies and critics who had been claiming that all his actions were aimed at personal and tribal military gains.

The Karzai government had not given in to pressure from human rights bodies who have been calling for a "truth commission" of sorts to be established with the goal to investigate "civil war" atrocities. Massoud's name has been brought up as well and we - who have actually known him - are worried that his name and legacy will be dragged through the dirt by people who do not understand any of his motifs, character or personality but are rather themselves to be accused of aspiring to egoistic goals. We congratulate Hamid Karzai for putting the stability of the country before pre-mature civil action in the matter. Of course, we are in favour of the true war criminals to be brought to justice, but investigations must be done in the right environment, within the right institutional framework and not end in a witch-hunt resulting in further destabilisation and disintegration of the country.

Further, any government should take care not to side-line those who have fought for the country in a long and enduring battle. By 2010 there appeared to have developed a trend to entrust most senior government positions with ethnic Pashtuns, while all representatives from other ethnic groups slowly but surely have been losing their influence and positions. The Panjshir Valley has been given province-status with 2 representatives to the Wolesi Jirga [Lower House of Parliament]. At the same time there is a sense among the northern minorities that they are increasingly labelled criminals, warlords, and gunslingers. Such a mood must be observed carefully and countered appropriately. They do not – after all – deserve any derogatory status after what they have achieved for the country.

Right from the beginning – from the day J.B. left Afghanistan – Massoud made it clear to his people – directly and indirectly – that I was under his personal command. In his absence I would follow Abdullah. Not knowing anything about nothing anyway I would not have hoped the situation to be otherwise and was very grateful for it. Like a new-born I had to learn everything from scratch: language mostly, who was who, the place of a woman here – all the rest of it appeared somewhat familiar and came easy to me. It helped tremendously of course to have two people with languages at their disposal which I spoke fluently. So, I never felt lonely or out of place. Slowly I grew into all my tasks, slowly I formed a picture of what was going on, what needed to be achieved, slowly I became part of this place.

Needless to say, my position was very special and only made possible by Massoud's personal intervention.

And he stood his ground. He felt I was a perfect addition to his endeavours for the following two reasons:

A foreign woman would – after a while and with proper guidance – be accepted as an "honorary man" among his men. As such I could realise many of his women related projects with direct access to the women concerned, without barriers.

Then, and very important to him, my knowledge of western languages and the fact that I was a westerner myself familiar with both cultures, made me an asset in dealing with the respective governments, agencies, and media.

He also wanted me to be his research unit. He wanted me to work closely with him on concepts of the new country that Afghanistan was supposed to become. For the latter I needed material. Interestingly enough, and quite revealing of the state that this country had slipped into, was the fact that an internet connection was easier to come by than books. We bought a satellite antenna from Iran and had it brought to Panjshir. There we actually managed to get an internet connection with broadband speed – it was quite amazing. I was never more grateful having brought my laptop along which I originally wanted to leave at home. At home? Home had surely become where the heart was.

Here I would draw material from the internet which Massoud asked me to gather. We often asked his brother Wali to get us books or magazines from overseas. Then he and I, often alone, sometimes with his close circle, would discuss aspects of civil governance and the institutions of a state. I compiled it all into documents on my PC and floppy discs – to be retrieved when they would become relevant, or to be fallen back on for implementation in the Panjshir. They never became relevant outside of the Panjshir – others designed and decided about the form and shape of the Afghan state.

In any case, it was an extraordinary thing to accept for these men that a woman was working among them every day. It was made possible only by Massoud and the position he commanded.

He returned to the Panjshir just an hour before J.B. left and from then onward, I was part of a world I did not know much about as far as daily detail was concerned.

After the helicopter took off, I boarded Massoud's land-cruiser. While he was sitting in front with a man called Jamshid, who was his brother-in-law, second-degree nephew and personal secretary, I sat on the backseat, watching the river with its willow-lined bank go by. At this point I was still not quite aware that my life had changed direction by one hundred and eighty degrees.

That same day in the late afternoon Massoud gathered all his commanders in his office in Saricha and introduced me to them. I sat next to his desk.

That office was a longish building and the meeting rooms in this one-storey building contain mainly sofas lined up along each wall. There he had a simple desk and swivel chair placed at the far end of one of the rooms, next to a window. The window behind him offered a far view across the mountains. The floor was covered with thin Afghan kilims and the whole building seemed to resemble a simple art-deco style.

Less than four years later his tomb would be some 500 metres from here, perched on the edge of a steep drop down to the river. His place on that little swivel chair would be taken by a huge bunch of fake flowers.

I am not a public speaker and I dislike a group of people looking at me like an exhibition piece. Luckily it was cold, so it was not uncomfortable to wear a big woollen dupatta [Hindi word for headscarf] covering my upper body and head, tightly closed at my neck, giving me psychological protection.

I would not say a word, I was not asked anything either. For minutes at a time, I would cover my nose and mouth with the cloth of my chador. Abdullah, sitting next to me, translated for me into English.

After Massoud explained who I was he said:

"Ariana is under my personal directive. She will be working on some of our projects in the Panjshir and together with Abdullah on international and press relations. She will also help us in planning the future of the Afghan state as she has seen different forms of statehood and has studied political science in the university in Germany. I am telling you all very clearly now that she is working for me. Her directives are my directives. She will be learning Dari and she is already very familiar with our culture.

This is a good training for you" he added with a smile. "In the society which we are fighting for women have the same rights as men, they are not men's subjects and subordinated so them. So, you better get used to listing to a woman occasionally." Though he laughed, I knew that he was serious.

Most of the men looked at me in a curious manner and nodded at Massoud's words.

After this introduction Massoud, Abdullah and myself left his office together while his men dispersed back to their tasks. The minute we left the house the satellite phone rang, and Abdullah went back in to receive the call. As a result, · Massoud and I had a minute to ourselves. His hands in his pockets he first looked at his boots, kicking a few small stones around, then raised his head and looked at me.

"How are you feeling?"

"Fine, Sahib – just fine." I looked back at him with my arms folded in front of my body. "Thank you for your kind words just now."

"You are welcome. Come let's take a walk." He turned around as Abdullah re-joined us and signalled me to follow. "Tomorrow, are you ready to start the battle?" he asked with a smile as we walked away from his office.

"As ready as I can get, I suppose" I smiled back at him.

"Good. Then tomorrow I will introduce you to some people involved with a school project. The headmistress speaks English so communication should not be a problem for you. I want you to take over from me there. Today I will brief you on what are the issues, what we want to achieve and so forth.

At the same time get started with your Dari, too. Abdullah will be there to help you."

As I would learn, this was just the tip of the iceberg in Massoud's methodical multi-layered thinking. He was an organisational masterpiece and I loved it.

"That sounds good" I looked at Abdullah. "Maybe we should set aside two hours every day for my Dari, what do you think?"

"Yes, no problem. Let me know when."

"O.k. – shall we say every morning at 9.00? We can sit in the Astana – is that o.k.? I am more of a morning worker."

"Yes, no problem. She is like you" he turned to Massoud "a plan in mind straight away ..." he smiled at his friend.

"That does not exactly sound like a compliment" Massoud teased him.

"You are free to interpret that whichever way you like – so I see you tomorrow, 9.00 am?" he turned back to me smiling, then walked away to board his car.

"Come, I bring you to the guesthouse – we can have dinner there and discuss the school project." Massoud finally said as we climbed into his land cruiser.

How I loved to spend time with him – I just so enjoyed his company, regardless of why we were together. Yet, or because of that and because I worried that he might never look at me the way I looked at him I always felt very insecure. I wanted to appear as knowledgeable and confident as possible so as not to disappoint him. At the same time, I was worried that I could never fulfil his expectations.

The gravel roads, the small fields with their stone-wall outlines, with some crops still standing, the little brown mud-brick houses ducking away into the landscape, all this was the Panjshir at this time of year.

The sun had almost set, Venus as the brightest star, lit up by the setting sun was already in the sky and it was getting chilli again.

"You must let me know if something is bothering you, tell me everything. Tell me what ever ideas you have, too, what you feel about what is going on around here etc. I want to hear your opinion on everything – is that alright? Don't be shy.

I feel we must work very closely to make all of this a success."

"I will. It may sound exaggerated yet, but please believe me that my heart is here, and I appreciate your confidence in me."

In the guesthouse we had dinner – the caretakers were already used to me not eating much meat so I would always get two vegetable dishes.

"Why do eat little meat?" he asked

"The wise men of India teach that meat has negative properties which keep the mind body-bound and makes it that much harder to gain higher levels of perception.

But also, in industrialised countries the slaughter of animals is something horrible. You should see, how, for example, cows are being kept in mass stables only to be slaughtered by machines. It is terrible. I hate to see animals suffer. They are so helpless and have done nothing to us."

"Actually, it's true – those who eat a lot of meat are unhealthy.

And I remember when I was a child, our Mullha in Jangalak used to tell us not to eat much meat. He, too, said that it was bad for you. Now I remember that. It is interesting, isn't it, this connection between what we eat and our state of mind."

After dinner we moved to the living room where they served us tea and we began talking about the mentioned school project. Again, I felt very insecure in his company, avoided his eyes after one or two seconds.

Despite my nerves I was looking for an opportunity to do something nice for him, something to show in a subtle manner that I ... well at least that I was happy to be here. This opportunity came when one of the caretakers wanted to serve us tea. I stopped him and signalled him not to serve us. Instead, I took the kettle and poured tea for Massoud.

"How much sugar do you take?" I asked him, raising my head.

"Two teaspoons". He smiled

"I give you your first Dari lesson today: Tashakor. That means Thank you."

"Tashakor" I replied, laughing, he smiling at me.

"How did you actually get to know J.B.? I never asked you" Massoud continued the conversation after a few seconds, stirring his tea.

After I told him - of course excluding the passion which had driven the endeavour - he said:

"You know, I only agreed for you to accompany him because it was him asking. Any other journalist I would have denied this request."

"So, I was very lucky …" I looked at him with a brief glance and then smiled into my teacup.

Since he left me, whenever I am pouring tea or coffee for other people, in my heart I am still serving him, I still feel his eyes resting on me.

After several weeks Massoud started inviting me to meetings. In the beginning when the men discussed among themselves, I usually stayed quiet, unless addressed directly – I would give my input, if I had any in the first place, to Massoud or Abdullah on other occasions, usually one on one. So, my mind sometimes wandered. I studied the men's faces or just thanked God for letting me experience all of this. Then slowly, as my Dari skills improved, I became part of those discussions.

While he was straight forward, energetic, and determined, sometimes to the degree of harshness when dealing with his men, he had otherwise such gentle ways, spoke softly and politely and his smile never failed to overwhelm me. And he always smiled and looked at me with a clear and open face, he gave me the feeling that no one else was in the room at that moment.

After several months I learned to read his intricate behaviour variances. I soon learned to read his eyes and body-language which, in subtle ways, communicated his true feelings which otherwise remained hidden from those who didn't know him well.

In the following weeks Massoud travelled a lot between Taloqan and the Panjshir. As a result, I did not see him for days upon end. Whenever he left, he gave me clear instructions on what I needed to accomplish by the time he got back.

As my involvement with the various projects intensified, he rang me often on the satellite phone when he was away. His office in Saricha was the only place with such a phone, so I used to take the calls there.

Sitting in his chair, at his desk, looking out of the window, seeing the willows move in the wind under the blue Afghan sky while talking to him has become such a deep memory for me.

So have those large Afghan window frames – three partitions and a small bottom window. Massoud's office had such windows, too. The frames were not air-tight so the curtains – sometimes tied up in a big knot - always moved slightly with the air coming through the gaps. This compliments my memory of those phone conversations as I always watched the curtains move while talking to him.

When he was in the Panjshir I met him almost every day to talk about all projects I was involved in. When we were done discussing official matters we spoke about many other things.

"What is happening with your business in Singapore. Did your partner find someone to replace you?" He asked me in

January 1998 as we settled down for tea in the Astana guesthouse one late afternoon to talk about a hospital project in Basarak. I was amazed: I only had told him once – in September of the previous year – that I was the co-owner of a business in Singapore.

"Yes, she found someone as an employee to take over my tasks. I am still the co-owner. No longer drawing a salary I am still on profit sharing so at the end of each year there should go some money into my account."

If it came to planning details of a project, it became clear very early in the day that we had a very similar mind – just like we thought very similar in matters of politics, religion, and many more which I had had the chance to discover already in October when I was still with the film crew.

For general modesty reasons and later of course to disguise our relationship, we never appeared on the scene of a project together. Since my projects mainly involved women-related matters it would have been inappropriate for him to be there anyway.

"O.k. – this is the latest plan for the hospital extension." I rolled open a sketch the engineer had drawn up for the women's hospital in Basarak.

"See, how they have changed the room arrangement at the south end? That way the access from the sterilisation unit to the wards is much shorter." I bent over to draw a line with my index finger.

"Yah, I can see that. That was a very good point Fatima brought up."

He was methodical, I was methodical – we knew what we wanted to achieve without many words. So, project management was what brought us close; extending this growing bond into times where we did not talk about official matters brought us closer over the weeks and months.

I noticed that he sought my company, he looked at me frequently, he often sought my opinion, even when in the company of his men and – when we were alone - he asked me often how I felt, how I was settling in, how my parents were doing and so forth. As the weather grew colder, he even showed concern for my physical well-being. When we were outdoors for longer periods of time, he sometimes asked whether I felt cold.

Our interaction was subtle and gentle, simply being comfortable with each other, full of easy respect. Our conversations were often filled with laughter.

So, after several weeks my trembling hands calmed down, my fluttering heart relaxed, and I started to enjoy every moment of his presence. I started to feel that I could keep up with his pace and that he was satisfied with my work. Step by step he gave me confidence by giving me my space among the men, by openly valuing my contributions.

I observed with excitement after a while that he seemed to feel more for me than just comfort. Sometimes during a conversation, he would look at me for this one or two moments longer than would have been necessary. Then he would smile and lower his eyes.

I never tried too hard but wanted to make my appearance as attractive as possible. Even though one is wearing a headscarf, long sleeve tops and baggy pants, one can still look very female. I always chose nice colours for my scarf, matching the rest of my clothes. My hair would always be tied up in the back and the scarf held in place by a pin. That way the scarf falls very nicely, giving the head a nice shape.

I always wore some make-up: the Indian kajal and mascara. Never too much, just subtle. When the sun was shining, I wore sunglasses which could be used for effect, too. I loved to slip them down to the tip of my nose and look at him over the rim.

I also often wore western men-style clothes. On such occasions I wore a big Pakul with all my hair stuffed under it. This gave a lot of freedom of movement as one didn't have to worry about the Chador coming lose and it also re-iterated my in-between position as a foreign woman.

After the winter-lull of 96/97, before which Massoud's forces and many refugees had retreated into the protective gorge of the valley, spring and summer were filled with defensive action and a major attack on the valley in spring 97 could be successfully repelled.

Concurrently Massoud sought to expand the resistance's unity and territorial coverage, so as to not be pinned down in the Panjshir by the enemy. He wanted to achieve that goal by first reaching out to General Rashid Dostum in a meeting in Pul-e-Khumri, a town some 100 kilometres south of the northern city of Kunduz along the main north-south artery which connects the Salang Pass with Kunduz and Mazar-e-Sharif. The six-hour meeting resulted in an understanding with this fickle ally and formed a first steppingstone to a more unified overall approach across the North in the years to come.

By early 1998 the flood of journalists who made their way to Northern Afghanistan to follow these developments had slowed to a trickle, after the initial Western public outcry over the Taliban's rule had somewhat subsided since they had taken power in late 1996.

While for most international media outlets the news cycle had moved on, during 1997 and 98 there were still a few more committed individuals who reported on the attempts of the Taliban to take the Panjshir.

So, some journalists did come on and off, and Massoud was always ready to give the requested interviews. He disliked the latter but bowed to the necessary. Of course, ever since I had been made in charge of his media relations, I encouraged him more and more to do interviews and take this opportunity to advertise his cause. Throughout my time assisting him with such matters there were only two or three cases in which he declined to see the person.

In February of 1998 there was a French lady-journalist, Marine Jacquemin, working for FTN who had come to Afghanistan to report on the origins and present situation of the Taliban rule. In the course of her work, she also came to the Panjshir to interview Massoud.

On a sunny cold morning Massoud met with a string of people one by one on various matters and afterwards made time for Marine and her team. They were all gathered in another of Massoud's offices in a side-valley and were getting ready to start the interview when I entered the room. His office desk there faces the door, so entering the room, after clearing a small woodstove, one will first look at the person sitting at the desk. When I walked through the door, he straight away caught my eyes and greeted me with a smile. I walked up to him, with all eyes on me.

"Salamaleikum. Khub astyn? Saat-e-taan khub?"

"Waleikum a salaam. Shukur."

He left the man he was dealing with standing while he turned his attention to me. I put some faxes on his table.

"These just came through."

I then turned to the journalist to apologise for barging in on her scene. I spoke to her in English first, then remembering that she was French I switched to her native tongue.

"I do apologise, but these papers need Amir Sahib's signature. I am Ariana, by the way, we spoke on the phone." I shook her hand and greeted the men in her team with my hand at my chest.

I turned back to Massoud.

"Thank you" he signed them all and raised his head "join us, please, when you are done." He said then turned to his man who, like a schoolboy, was patiently waiting for his turn.

"I will." With that I rushed out of the room, holding my colourful chador at the left side so it would not fly off my head. The one thing I did never bowed to was to dress in dull colours. In summer I would wear my Panjabi Suits all the time. Long sleeves, but with pastel-colour thin chiffon chadors. Even when I got winter clothes tailored there, I still picked nice colours. I was not a widow yet, was I? As far as I am aware nobody complained about it either. If someone had, I know that Massoud would not have entertained him as he never was a friend of any strict dress codes – strict meaning in the Islamic sense of the word, not the Western. However, me living there permanently he would not have tolerated me not wearing a headscarf or always covering my arms when in public and other such conventions.

When I returned, I thought the interview would be already underway, but it seemed that he had made only small talk, making them wait until I came back.

There was no chair left so I went to stand behind Massoud's desk.

"Bring one more chair" Massoud immediately turned to one of his aides. Then only did I notice Abdullah in the corner, next to the window. Just about to sit down I rose again and apologised to him, while shaking his hand.

I then pulled the chair closer and Marine began by speaking to Massoud in French. He replied as well as he could. Talking of political, military, and economic matters requires a different language level compared to what our daily interactions were comprised of.

She suggested then that she pose the questions in French to him and have him reply in Dari, translated by the television team's own translator, but made it clear that she much preferred it if he spoke in French. It appeared to me that, by pressuring him to speak French, she had some agenda. She seemed to believe that by speaking in French his true intentions would come out rather than having his words "disguised" by a translator. From the beginning I found that annoying. What was the point?

Of course, like many female journalists attempting to engage with Afghanistan, she had a female-rights agenda, overshadowed by her Western upbringing, which did not consider the cultural sensitivities of this country.

She had come dressed fairly casually: no headscarf, sleeves barely reaching her joints, short winter jacket and short pull-over. Luckily it was still rather cold, so she wore a sweater with a turtleneck and a wind breaker. Some of these journalists thought that just because Massoud was a moderate Muslim, all Muslim values could go out of the window altogether. I therefore later suggested to Massoud to let all female journalists know in advance that they were expected to dress according to local minimum standards so as to not give the wrong image to his men and also not to let him appear to be approving of such things. He agreed and from there onward I would include a list of dress code recommendations into the paperwork that preceded any press visits to our territory.

Before she began, she turned to me and asked what I was doing here, whether I was a journalist, too.

"No, I am not. I live here, trying to help this cause, trying to end the Afghan Tragedy."

"She is not only helping, she is doing an incredible job." Massoud added, smiling at me.

Embarrassed I lowered my head and smiled, too, then looked back at him.

"You are helping in warfare – is that an appropriate place to be in for a woman. Should you not be working for peace?"

I looked at her with a question mark in my eyes. It took me a second to catch on with this provocative question.

"See, sometimes one has to take up weapons to forge peace. Not every conflict can be solved Gandhi's way. These people refuse negotiations. They and their proxies refused to share power with Amir Sahib's party simply because they resent his leadership as a Tajik, and as a person. They also are fundamentally opposed to his vision for this country and a tolerant Islam. How do you deal with that? We have repeatedly offered negotiations with the Taliban – they were all rejected. Are we supposed to walk to the guillotine voluntarily?"

"She is right – that is exactly the point." Massoud added looking at me with a smile. He always got amused when I talked in a passionate fashion.

"The situation that we are in calls for resistance – we have no other choice." He added in a serious manner.

"Anyway, shall we begin" Massoud turned to Marine in French. And once more he was asked the questions, he had answered many times before, coming to the same conclusions as before. Urging the West to stop supporting Pakistan and their backers and many more.

This was the first time that I was part of an interview with Massoud. It was the first time I was part of the scenario, the first time my position here became an issue of questions. All his verbal support was mine, all his body language told me that he appreciated me being here.

When he answered the questions, as always passionate and dedicated, I watched him all the time, sipping my tea.

His face was so expressive when he spoke. Again, some people would have called it harsh. As soon, however, as he switched to casual conversation his face relaxed

I was so glad to be here. This was part of the purpose I was here for: to talk to the world, to get our message out there. Sometimes he looked at me.

He would be at his thinnest at that time, his cheeks were quite hollow, but his face as animated as always. We would look more filled out from 1999 onward, but that is when he started to age, too.

As it had become my habit, I would re-fill the teacups, refill the nut-trays. To serve him, to serve this country made me happy. It still does – just now there is a hole in my heart which cannot be filled.

When asked about the readiness of his troops to fight back the Taliban offensives he pointed out that he had an elite force in place that was willing to sacrifice themselves for this cause and fight until their last breath.

"What about you?" Marine turned to me. "How resolute are you? Will you give your life here, if necessary?"

"Yes" I replied without hesitation "this is my life now. If our men must die for what we believe in, we must be ready to die, too. And I will do everything for and with Amir Sahib; that includes dying with him." I gave him a quick, serious glance.

"But this is not your country – how have you become so involved here?"

"Afghanistan has grabbed my attention for many years. And I have followed Amir Sahib's struggle for at least a decade. I had always wanted to meet him and when I had the opportunity to do so last year, I jumped at it. What I saw impressed me very, very much and I had finally found my purpose. This cause is worth any fight because it cares about humanity."

Again, Massoud looked at me. But this time he did not smile. He looked at me in a serious, attentive manner. After I finished, he continued to look at me for a moment. These were the breathless seconds which to me communicated such closeness between us. Unspoken closeness. Just complete understanding and appreciation.

Marine's questions had not much substance, nothing that was not asked before, nothing that showed any in-depth knowledge of the country and political situation.

Massoud therefore moved to end the interview quickly and got up. While getting ready to walk out of the room Marine again questioned him why he did not want to reply to her in French.

"How much of my questions did you understand in French?" she asked

"About 60 percent"

"Why then do you not reply to me in French. It would make things that much easier."

"It is a bit difficult for me and also there are not many people here who speak French."

Smiling, he, Abdullah and I walked out of his office and headed for a small wooden house across the road.

And then it got lots worse:

While we walked across the road, she caught up with us and shouted from maybe ten metres away:

"Commander, commander, can I just ask you one last question?"

Massoud turned around in his lovely, patient way, laughing.

"You have fought now for twenty years. Isn't it enough? Reply to me in French, please!"

Had I not completely been out of line, I would have said something, but of course chose to watch the scene from the entrance door of the house we were about to step into.

"It is a bit difficult for me" he repeated in French and then turned to the interpreter to answer the question.

"As we have told you earlier, we want peace, no doubt, but not at any price. This is a matter of defending our homeland. We will fight for our values until our last breath."

While he was speaking in Dari to the interpreter, who first asked him whether he had understood the question, which he said he had, she interrupted him twice, urging him to speak in French. He was too patient, but now I could see a tinge of irritation as he did not look at her anymore while giving the reply. He simply interrupted her and continued addressing the interpreter. That shut her up. After she had the reply translated, all she said was: "Aha".

He then turned to shake everybody's hands, saying "merci, salam maleikum" and then disappeared inside the house. Moving aside to let him pass I stepped out and caught up with Marine as she was about to leave.

"Marine – I am sorry, can I have a quick word with you?"

"Sure"

"At the end of the day I cannot tell you what to do, but please consider not speaking to Amir Sahib like this again. You were about to overstep a line here. This is not the way. He does not owe you anything, he can speak in any language he pleases, and he does not cover up anything by speaking in Dari. If you were really interested in Afghanistan and the culture you would pick up some Dari and then come back and speak to him again – in his language." I looked at her for a second, then turned around to join Massoud.

"Ariana – if his values are anything to go by, he will tolerate such things."

"He is tolerating it, as you can see, just like he is tolerating that you are not covering your hair, but there is something the West has lost – decency and respect. And no one deserves respect more than this man. Not everything must be sacrificed on the altar of journalism, free speech, and such things, do you understand?" I turned once more to leave.

"Why do you defend things that are against women's rights?"

"Marine – what have I defended that is against women's rights? Just because I tell you to cover your head in line with the culture here does not mean I am against our rights. You know, you can be a respected woman with equal rights to men and still keep a religiously routed dignity. That is, what most European women do not understand." I began to lose patience.

Not replying to my outburst, she changed the topic:

"What is your relationship with Massoud? How are you able to live and work here?"

"Do not even start, o.k. – let things be, please. I told you what I am doing here. There is nothing to add. Have a save trip back – Khuda Afiz!"

With that I stepped into the house and shut the door.

Abdullah and Massoud looked at me when I stepped in, both with a smile on their face – they had heard every word.

"You should become one of my bodyguards" Massoud laughed at me "Your words cut deeper than any bullet."

"I am sorry, Sahib" I replied looking at him, embarrassed. I had stuck my head out too far, like many times in my life.

"No, no – do not apologise. That was the right thing to say." He smiled at me. "Please sit. We have more important things to turn to now."

On May 1st that same year I sat in my room in the Astana guesthouse with my laptop. I remember it to be May 1st because I had just read on the BBC website about some labour demonstrations in Europe.

It was the hours of the generator, so I made full use of it, including running my disc man on its speakers. Listening to the music while I was working, I tapped the table in imaginative tabla fashion. My little desk faced the windows, so I would sit with my back towards the door.

Massoud would knock of course before he entered my room but, on that day, I did not hear his knock as I played the music quite loudly. So, when I suddenly saw him standing next to me, I almost literally jumped off my chair.

"My God, you startled me – I did not hear you at all" I stared at him. "Salam, Sahib" I added with a calmer voice bringing my right hand to my chest, then lowering the volume of the music.

"Salam, Ariana. I knocked but you would not hear. So, since I heard your music play, I figured you must be in … so I just went in. – You should play percussions, you tab your "tablas" very well" he joked, sitting down in the only other chair in my room

"Oh no, you wouldn't want to hear that – I have the worst sense of rhythm. I just know the Bhangra beat so well that even I can tap it."

"Anyway" he found the escape "I did not come here to discuss music with you, even though of course I did not mind" he paused, scratching his right temple, and smiled at me, realising what trap he had talked himself into.

"Yes ...?" I replied in a cocky fashion, one eye on my computer.

"You know what I mean." He smiled his most beautiful smile and had an embarrassed look in his eyes.

"I wanted to talk to you about what you should be doing in the next week. You know that I am starting a trip to Teheran and Herat tomorrow, right?"

"Yes, of course. – Let me get some tea and we will talk about it." I got up, and with a swift hand movement moved my scarf and hair behind my right ear while standing and looking at my computer screen as I closed one document I was working on. That way he got to see one of the little dangling earrings I was wearing, of course matching the colour of my chador. I turned around, gave him a little smile, and walked out to call for some tea.

When I returned, I settled back into my chair and grabbing a notepad and a pen I looked at him.

"Alright, so what do you have in mind?"

Then, as was his habit, his face suddenly turned serious, and we finally started talking about the things he came to see me for ...

Nessun Dorma[10]

"Ed il mio bacio scioglierà il silenzio
Che ti fa mia"[11]

8th May 1998

I had been in Taloqan, the capital of Takhar Province, for two days.

The compound of the Northern Alliance local headquarters there was composed of several buildings. The Tajik border is only about seventy kilometres north of here.

Taloqan itself was a small provincial town of about 150,000 people at the time. It was green, with many tree-lined roads. A traditional rural Afghan town.

In Taloqan Massoud had provided me with a small house all to myself with a living room which doubled up as bedroom during the night, a small kitchen, and a small bathroom.

"Bathroom" in Afghanistan consists mostly of a squat toilet and a wash basin. I always had the feeling that I was the one buying up all toilet paper available in the bazaars as this was not a common thing to use at the time. "Rinsing" was the order of the day, something I could never live with! - Awful, rough and single-layered, the pink Pakistani toilet paper was better than nothing, though.

---

[10] Aria "Nobody shall sleep" from the Puccini opera "Turandot"
[11] "And my kiss will break the silence, which makes you mine"

"Showers" were bucket showers. Regular showers require electricity for everything: for heating the water somewhere in a boiler and for pumping it. Without a functioning power grid this was not possible. So, one resorted to immersion coils, when the generator was running and heated up a bucket of water. Once it was hot, one would scoop the water over oneself with a large plastic cup. It always amazed me how much one could do with 10 litres of water! In winter I got very fast with all of this: strategic and timely removal of clothes and maximum use of the steam the bucket shower created in a small bathroom to keep warm, before drying off and putting my clothes back on. One had to be careful, too, that the plastic handle of the immersion coil wasn't broken in any way, otherwise an electric shock was the result.

It was a bit chilly that evening, that May 8th in 1998, almost ten o'clock and I was sitting at my desk in what we called "the office". During these last few months, I had to get used to "winter" again after living in the tropics for 5 years. I must have always worn at least two layers more than everybody else.

"The office" was a large room in one of the houses draped with simple window dressings and laid out with carpets, three desks, several chairs and a sitting area with floor cushions in one corner. This was where I did most of my work, where we, as in the Panjshir, had a satellite system installed which enabled us to access the internet and have phone and fax connections. This was one of the costliest investments we made. But it was absolutely critical for our communication ability.

We had one electric light bulb hanging from the ceiling. It almost seemed that we had run out of cash for a better light source after installing the satellite system.

All that could of course only be operated when the diesel generator was running. When the generator was off, we had kerosene lamps everywhere else.

This is where I had been studying Dari for the last few months under the skilful guidance of Abdullah. Mastering the alphabet was the hardest – after that the language turned out to be less challenging than I had thought. As very few people in the camp spoke anything but Dari I had "direct immersion" making it easier for me to acquire a basic level of the language.

My desk was looking out through a high window onto the orchard behind the house. As it was spring the trees started to carry fresh green leaves and the view onto the mountains became more and more obstructed as the foliage increased.

A walkway was leading by that window, so unless someone came in from across the empty field on the other side, I would notice him.

That was what happened that evening when Massoud returned after a one-week absence. He had undertaken the above-mentioned trip to Teheran to appeal for vital support for the Northern Alliance. Cut off from Pakistani supplies after the civil war, the failed Peshawar and Islamabad Accords and all personal tensions between Hekmatyar and Massoud, Iran was a supporting ally at the time

Whenever he was gone for longer, I missed him and could not wait for him to return. Whenever he was engaged in battle activity, I had to force the thoughts out of my mind that I might have seen him for the last time.

Massoud had made it a point for Abdullah to look after me in his absence. So, he and I had plenty of time to discuss all matters we were involved in at length. Abdullah is a quiet individual, very intelligent, western educated and deep thinking. He was the man in the background, spinning his wheels and connections. He never struck me as a commander, always much more as a politician. Already in those days I thought he would be well suited to be a minister in a future all-Afghan government.

Finally, I saw Massoud walk past with a few men in his trail, as would normally be the case. He hardly ever had the luxury of being alone anywhere. It was his typical silhouette: his army boots, his pants tucked into them, his pakul tilted to the right, his hands in his pockets and a spring in his step. He would always look groomed; he would never look untidy, whether he wore western or Afghan clothes, whether he was relaxed or whether his face told of worries or strain.

And that it did often. During those few years I would see the immense burden he carried grey his hair in parts - particularly above his left temple - and engrave his face with lines. Especially when the enemies advanced on his territory, when the Europeans listened politely but substantial help was not forthcoming; especially in his last year the exhaustion was clearly written on his face, his hair had turned even more grey. Sometimes, after we returned from Europe in April 2001, looking at his still so handsome face I felt a knife cut through my heart. I had never seen anyone with his endurance and will to succeed against all odds, yet even this extraordinary man was at the verge of disenchantment. How I wanted to give him the victory and peace he craved!

Talking to one of the men he was turning his back to me when he passed by the window, so I thought he had not noticed me. As he was not alone, I did not think he would come in as he would usually come here only by himself to gather his thoughts, write in his diary, or read his poems.

Anyway, I was engrossed in my plan on how to approach the foreign media, on how to tackle the Western attention to Afghanistan's plight and how to, that way, tackle the Taliban. I wanted to have an initial plan laid out in a few days' time to present it to Massoud and Abdullah.

So focused was I on my drafts that evening that I did not hear Massoud come into "the office" after all.

"Why are you still working?" I suddenly heard the beloved voice behind me.

Taken aback, I swivelled around and looked at him. Smiling, I said:

"I just wanted to make some progress on these press issues. - How is the Herat front keeping up and how did things go with Rafsanjani?" I asked after a second.

"I will brief you all tomorrow about the Iranian matter. As far as Herat is concerned: Not too well, the boys there need a lot more training. The Taliban is re-grouping over there it appears, so things are not too bad yet. But we need to be far better prepared. Most of the fighters there are quite young. I put Bismillah Khan in charge. He will be able to pull it off. You know how tough he can be with his boys ..."

"Yah, I have seen it. I guess that type of man is necessary in that type of circumstances."

He stood next to me and picked up the Dari book which I had been studying with during the last few months. He leafed through the already quite worn pages.

"How are you?" he asked in Dari

"I am fine." I replied

Then he turned and leaned against the desk, not more than a foot away and began reading one of the texts.

"Translate into French for me" he demanded, looking at me with a candid expression in his eyes.

I did as told.

"You are doing fine" he put down the book with a satisfied expression. Then he looked at me for a long moment and his face turned serious, then he looked away, down at his hands which he kept folded in his lap.

Two more seconds of silence.

I do not know what besieged me at that moment, but it must have been my extreme, bottled-up affection for him finally bursting its cork. But also, it appeared to me very strongly at that moment that he was waiting for me to do or say something of a personal nature.

So, I moved my right hand towards him, touched his arm. His beige sweater felt so soft, he looked so handsome as always.

He did not move away, nor did he shrug. He just looked at me and I looked at him. He then put his left hand onto mine as it rested on his right arm.

"Please do not do this. I cannot. You know that I cannot."

"What do you expect me to do? You must know what I feel for you. If you say, you do not know, you are lying to me. If you tell me, you do not feel the same for me, you are lying even more."

A moment of silence. He looked at me, then took my hand.

"Do you know how tempted I am right now, how tempted I have been for months. Do you know that?

Yes, I have fallen for you, more than I can put into words - but I have a family!"

How his sentence excited and hurt me at the same time!

"If that is the case, please don't force yourself to break my heart. I could not bear it.

We are the same in mind and soul. How can you throw something like this away?"

"You know my answer, but you also know my situation." He got up, stood behind me, slipped off my headscarf and stroked my hair, my cheeks - then simply walked out.

"'If you can't stay in front of my eyes – then leave my heart, too.' Do you remember? Now you are doing exactly that to me. Impossible love. Thing is, I won't leave your heart!" I turned around in a half-loud voice, reminding him of the Quawali song and the evening of music we had shared in October last year.

He stopped dead in his path, turned around and looked at me, with lines crossing his forehead. For a second there he seemed undecided whether to move on or turn around.

"Please do not do this to me. Please." He said quietly, turned around and left.

What followed was the most horrible week of my life. I felt as if the roof had collapsed onto my head. The man I loved more than life had decided for his family. Within five minutes all built up illusions had burst like soap bubbles. This is what J.B. had warned me about!

I could not sleep; I could not work. I did everything in slow motion. Everything passed by in a daze; I did things in an automated fashion. At night I cried my heart out. I did not know what to do.

Yet I could not bring myself to give Massoud the cold shoulder, much less simply walk out of this. I understood where he was coming from, I knew now that he felt for me like I felt for him, but he was too much of a man to outright give in to his feelings because his conscience was haunting him. This beautiful part of his character made it even worse for me: it drew me even more to him, falling in love even more with that man who was not only attractive in mind, body, and soul, but who was also ridden by a bad conscience and ready to suffer for it.

I continued working with him but was too sad and disappointed to laugh with him and smile at him, reciprocate his gaze even. When our eyes met, I quickly looked away. In meetings I became very quiet, pulling my chador over my mouth. When he addressed me, my answers were short and gave only the absolutely relevant information.

One week later I sat on the floor cushions in the office. I had asked dinner to be brought to me there. Waiting for the food sadness overcame me so much that I had to cry. Just sitting there, I stared into a corner. What was I going to do? Love had burst my heart but the man I had fallen for did not want to allow it.

When the aid brought the food, I moved to the desk which was overlooking the orchard. While flipping through some papers I ate.

Then, at around eight o'clock the door opened and Massoud walked in.

"Ça va, ma chère?" [how are you, my dear] He asked in French.

His words swamped my heart! - Did he just say that?

Yet I replied in a wilful manner: "Non, ça n'va pas, pas du tout" [not well, not well at all], close to tears. I did not even turn around to look at him.

Then I felt his hands on my shoulders.

Before I could realise what was going on, he brushed my hair from the left side of my neck to the other.

"I am sorry that I hurt you. I am so sorry. I was trying to be rational, but I cannot.

I cannot bear what our relationship has slipped into over the last week. I see your sad face and my heart hurts.

I thought of your words that we are the same in mind and soul and that I am throwing this away.

I feel the same way - that is the thing; you warm my heart; you excite me in so many ways. And even though I should, I can't send you away from my heart."

I closed my eyes and put my right hand onto his left, which was still resting on my shoulder.

Then he turned the swivel chair I was sitting on in his direction so that I faced him. I looked into his beautiful eyes, and we smiled at each other. "I cannot bear to lose you."

He caressed my cheek with his right hand.

Then, grabbing my hands he pulled me out of the chair.

"Come let's go. Please turn off the lamps".

I locked the door behind us, and we walked towards my house.

We walked into the empty night with the almost full moon lighting up the way, giving the trees an eyrie look. I felt like taking his hand and putting it around my waist, but of course I did not. I felt so excited. There are only few moments in your life when you feel you are exactly where you want to be. This was one of them. My heart was beating up to my throat as the rubble squeaked under our feet.

Without saying another word, we arrived at my door. I opened it and we entered – no questions asked.

First thing I did was reach for the kerosene lamp and matches to light it.

"I hope I did not offend you just now" he said with a boyish look in his eyes, half leaning against half sitting on my kitchen table as the light lit up his face, exacerbating his sharp features.

"Oh no, not at all, why would you? – you took me by surprise, but you have made me very happy. You woke me from the daze I have been in over the last week. I was so sad, that I cannot describe it to you" I replied, first smiling at him, then nervously avoiding his gaze while fidgeting with my door key as it did not want to come out from the lock.

"I have been wishing for this to happen for months, for years, ever since I have known about you. But I never dared to hope for it." I put the key onto the table looking at him, just standing there for a second.

He put his pakul onto the table.

And then he reached out, pulled me close and kissed me. Soft and tender at first, then more passionate. I ran my hands through his thick hair.

With his arms tightly around my waist, mine around his neck, my heart started to race; I couldn't breathe!

An erotic wave washed over me as he led me to my bed.

"My Goodness, what are you doing to me?" he said some time later, laying on his back with his right arm over his eyes.

I laughed.

Then he rolled onto his side, resting his upper body on his left arm, and looked at me. "You mustn't forget that I'm pushing fifty."

"And what? That makes you an old man? – Didn't feel like that to me ..."

"Hmm" he smiled. "I'm glad to hear it."

"Can you promise me something?" he asked while we were still lying on my bed with two blankets covering us.

"That depends" I replied in an insecure manner, suddenly fearing that he might say something along the lines of "nobody must know about this, we can't repeat this".

"Promise me to never leave my side until the day I die. I will never want to miss your company."

"I have been in love with you from the day I learned about you. Ever since I met you in person your life has become my life, your cause has become my cause and I have never felt for anyone the way I am feeling for you ... so, yes, I promise. - Can you promise the same to me, though?" I reluctantly removed the blanket and grabbed my clothes. While I put them on as quickly as possible, he replied:

"I promise." looking me straight in the eyes.

Had I known at that moment that it would only take three and a half more years until we would be released of that promise, I would not have moved from his side one single day. Thinking that it would be many more years for death to part us we were often separated for days, sometimes for weeks. I was not with him for a few days before they murdered him. So not keeping my promise left me alone and deserted, while otherwise I might have had the chance to die with him.

"You know, I had thought of approaching you for a few weeks now but always my reason held me back, I covered my thoughts with all the work I have, I tried not to let them get into my brain because I have a wife and children. I tried to escape all this, but I could not. When I saw the pain in your eyes last week, I started feeling that same pain. I could suddenly not imagine that we would not love each other.

I know that I am contravening pretty much every law and convention there is. But I never thought that I would ever fall in love the way I have," he walked over to the window where I was standing and caressed my hair. "In fact, until I became aware of my feelings for you, I did not believe that such strong emotions even really existed or even that they could ever eclipse the feelings for my wife. I was actively resisting thinking of you. For a few days I even avoided you – I don't know whether you noticed. I thought I should have never allowed you to stay. But I love to spend time with you." He paused, put his left hand to my chin and kissed me.

"Do you remember a few days before J.B. and your camera crew left, when you were playing all those songs? I think this was the evening when I fell in love with you, totally irrationally and completely forgetting my situation. But your spirit and temperament became so clear that night and that's when it struck me that you are the woman I want. But I knew that you were going to leave again, and I was aware of the impossibility of this situation. So here already I pushed these thoughts out of my mind.

When J.B. then told me that you wanted to stay on to get involved with our cause I could not believe my ears. While all alarm bells of reason were ringing inside of me, I gave in and said that you could stay."

We sat down on the floor cushions.

"I will tell you now what happened that morning:

He came to my house and sat down for breakfast with me. I was surprised because for all that while he had not done so. Then after a few minutes he asked me whether we could speak in private. After I sent everyone else away, he said:

'Ariana asked me to ask you something: straight forwardly: she has been very, very impressed with your efforts here and everything which is going on. In fact, I should tell you that she has followed your struggle for the last decade. Hence she would like nothing more but to stay on here and work for you.'

I looked at him in surprise.

'Are you serious?' I asked him and then after my inner voice of buried feelings for you and a rational assessment of the advantages you bring won the battle, I told him that we could give this a try. And I gave him all the reasons which are known to you.

'Are you very sure that you want to allow her to stay?' J.B. asked then. 'Despite of what you have just said not only might things shape up to be very difficult for her here to be accepted but more importantly I am worried that your reputation will suffer as you will agree with me that she is not exactly unattractive, right?'

'Yes, I agree with you' I replied 'but the only thing I am seeing right now is that she could do a lot of things for us, don't you think so? Other than that, I can handle it.'

Well, I couldn't handle it as you can see. And I was lying to myself when I told J.B. otherwise." He smiled in an innocent manner as I got up to start a fire in the bukhari. I must have been the only one still having a wood oven up by May, but I took the luxury of still heating on a cool night like these.

"Most people will say I should not have done what I did today, but I made a conscious decision because I have been totally overwhelmed by you as I got to know you better. Your passion for our cause is one reason. I could not believe your dedication, the effort and energy you put up! Really."

He joined me at the bukhari, took a spate from my hand and kissed me again. "And you have an understanding for our culture and what is going on politically that eclipses many local peoples' knowledge. The people realise that. Initially I was concerned of course that you might not be able to settle in well into this unfamiliar world and that you might not be accepted as a woman having something to say. But you have proofed everybody wrong."

"Do you think that your commanders see it the same way?"

"Yes, almost all of them. Of course, wanting to be popular with everybody is not attainable. If I wanted that I should have given up long time ago. There will always be people who are only with you as long as their little egoistic needs are taken care of. As soon as you can't cater to them anymore, they will drop you like a hot potato. But as long as you are aware of that, you can make use of them.

I will protect you by not bringing you along to meetings where those people who might be opposed to you are present. There are very few indeed, and they do not belong to my close circle. Don't worry about that for the moment."

"I am very glad that it turned out that way."

He paused.

"You are such an amazing dichotomy to me: you look European, but your speech, demeanour, beliefs and convictions are oriental and so close to mine that I see myself in you. At the same time, you are a strong spirited character, in many ways equal to men. Something I have never experienced in a woman. You make me want to protect you but at the same time I know you can take care of yourself.

I never thought of a woman to be able to satisfy a man on all levels. With you I feel alive, I feel I can discuss everything, share everything, and get input which challenges me.

When I first met you down in the Panjshir I felt immediately drawn to you. I had no notion yet why and how, but I liked you from the start. Not only that – I was struck by your appearance. You looked very pretty that day - as you always do. When J.B. walked me over to where you were standing, I thought to myself: 'who is this beautiful woman?' – I first thought you were Afghan, but then I remembered that J.B. had said that you were German. When you greeted me in Afghan style I was surprised because I did not expect a German lady to know all these things; and then when you removed your sunglasses and I saw your green kajal-lined eyes I was spoken to as a man - subconsciously yet, but still. Now looking back, I see all this very clearly.

See, therefore our traditions dictate to hide women behind a cover because we are afraid of their beauty." [12]

He smiled, then pulled me close and kissed me.

---

[12] Massoud was often questioned why his wife, too, wore the Chadori. But one must understand that these are religiously routed traditions kept to by all country-women in Afghanistan. Only in the cities many women do away with that body-engulfing cover.

"I should be afraid, too, but I am telling myself this: God is love and if we love each other, we are not contravening God, are we?"

"Yes, I agree. Sometimes life is not straight forward. Of course, many people would not agree."

Again, J.B. had been right. Years later he told me that he thought Massoud liked me straight away when he introduced us. He said that having known him for many years, and hence knowing how he behaved towards people, he thought that his eyes rested on me for just one or two seconds longer than would have been necessary when I turned away from him to walk towards those cars.

"I am so very happy right now; I can't even tell you. But I do not want to end up heartbroken; I do not want to fall victim to your bad conscience.

I will not get in your way, on any level, but I would wish for you to keep the promise you just made. If you leave me by the roadside one day, I will not survive it well, or not at all, please know that."

"I promise you. I won't break your heart – not voluntarily, not if I can avoid it with all means in my power.

You must understand this: When I got married I did so because I thought it might otherwise be too late – I was already 34 then.

And even though we have five children, and my wife is a lovely, good, and caring woman, our relationship is not based on that sort of strong attraction. I must tell you, I do love her but not in the manner I feel for you. At the same time, I always wanted to have a family. That was the main reason why I got married."

At that moment I was surprised and grateful that he had brought up this issue, something which I had banished from my thoughts ever since I knew how I felt about him

"However," he continued "I cannot offer you to make our relationship official – ever. That I hope you are clear about? That does not mean that I do not value you or that I will ever disrespect you in any way. But it would be very, very hard ..."

"I totally understand." I interrupted him. "As long as you keep your earlier promise, I will be happy." He smiled at me and stroked my head.

After that we did not touch on the issue anymore. He would go to be with his family at his discretion. For security reasons nobody, except two or three people of his closest circle knew at any one time the whereabouts of his family.

The reader may wonder why I accepted such a status. Surely if he had really loved me the way he claimed would he not have wanted to marry me, particularly as a Muslim who was allowed to have up to four wives?

The fact was that matters would have turned out to be very complicated and destructive, not least because I was a foreigner and not a Muslim.

We did not aim at having children; we did not want to be a family. All we wanted was share each other's company until each other's death because we felt that we were soulmates, even though part of his attention and emotions were with his wife and children. The fact that we were living in a society and situation which would have never accepted and understood that we just left our official relationship the way it had been presented to everyone else and were content with having carved out that special space for us. Had I not been one hundred percent sure that he reciprocated my deep feelings I would not have continued this relationship after a while. A perception of being taken advantage of will kill even the deepest feelings. And he never gave me reason to feel that way.

His diary-entry on May 9th, 1998, read:

Last night I broke Allah's law. Yet I have never felt so happy in a long time. Today I loved the woman He sent me from out of nowhere. It has become impossible for me not to think of her. She makes my heart light and happy. She is beautiful. She reflects my heart, my soul – I love her company. Her words are my thoughts. How beautiful it was to touch her, to kiss her, to finally be with her.

The fact that he was married and the thought that he even remotely loved another woman has, however, always stayed a sour point in my heart.

Even more so the fact, that he would have another child with his wife after we started our relationship.

He knew that this hurt me and when it happened, he came to tell me and made a special effort to re-assure me of his love for me, convinced me of our special bond but at the same time stressing that he could not simply abandon his wife.

I remember it was in early August 1998 that he knocked on my door one late evening. From his face I could tell that he had bad news of sorts. Worried, I urged him to come in:

"Come – what happened – you look worried!"

Walking through the door he began:

"Do you believe that I love you? As much as you love me? Search your heart and tell me the truth." He sat down.

"Yes, of course, I do believe that." I sat next to him, taking his hand.

"And I really do – I swore to you, remember? I never want you to forget this!" His voice sounded a bit shaky. "Tell me that you will never forget this."

"I won't forget it." I replied, getting more worried with each word.

"Good." He paused looking straight at me, hesitant to continue. "Despite that I will have to hurt you now, but I have no choice."

My heart sank, my stomach panicked.

"My wife is pregnant."

I just looked at him in disbelieve and let go of his hand.

Then a quiet sadness settled onto me, and I turned away from him. I suddenly felt second-best. I felt pushed away from him.

He just kept sitting there, looking at me as I sat with my arms wrapped around my knees and my head resting on them, tears of frustration running down my face.

After I recovered from my first anger, I remembered the words we had exchanged just before that and then turned my head and asked him:

"Is she fine? How many months already?"

"She is fine. Three months."

"Forgive me for my selfish reaction" I finally said, turning back towards him "But I just love you too much in order not to feel jealous."

"Of course – I know. That is why I told you what I told you before. What we have is above everything else, beyond compare. Yet I can't abandon her. She is the mother of my children and when I married her, I made a commitment to her.

So, some months ago – three months ago, apparently – she told me that she wanted to have another child. What was I to say? It was, by the way, if that comforts you, a few days before we got together."

"I understand – please forgive me. And yes, that does make a difference to me."

"No, no, there is nothing to forgive. I understand you, too. You are giving everything to me, I have your total commitment in our love and in our struggle, but you must share me, in a way. I am not sure if I could do the same if it were the other way around. This is just one of the things I so much appreciate about you. So please try to understand. You should know by now how I feel about you. I am not taking advantage of you. Please believe me."

"What if I fell pregnant one day?" I asked him after a few seconds

"You would make me very, very happy."

"How would you explain it?"

"I don't know, but there is always a way."

Oh, God how I loved him – I reached out and took his hand again. What a situation to be in – but I would have never chosen a different path. I am too much of a Scorpio: passion, heartbreak and dedication characterise us. Flying high, lying low, drinking from the cup of life till its last drop!

In retrospect I have been wondering whether it was a coincidence that Sadiqa wanted to have another child with her husband at that time. Did she learn about our close relationship? And knowing that she could not do anything about it tried to extend the bond with her husband that way?

I will never know, but it was very re-assuring to see that Massoud was shaken by this and that he spoke to me the way he had.

Thinking about his words I eventually came to accept and understand what I meant to him: I had nothing to do with his family, I was his muse in whose company he could be completely himself, find his match in spirit and body, could be free and happy. To me he could talk about everything, get challenged and be supported like by a male friend; yet at the same time we were man and woman, we were attracted to each other on all levels possible.

He let me feel in his gentle ways how much he loved me. In the way he kissed me, in the way he looked at me in the way he trusted me with his cause, in the way we worked together, in the things he told me, in the way he spoke to me – it was in all that, that he showed me.

A moment of happiness,
you and I sitting on the veranda,
apparently two, but one in soul, you and I.
We feel the flowing water of life here,
you and I, with the garden's beauty
and the birds singing.
The stars will be watching us,
and we will show them
what it is to be a thin crescent moon.
You and I unselfed, will be together,

indifferent to idle speculation, you and I.
The parrots of heaven will be cracking sugar
as we laugh together, you and I.
In one form upon this earth,
and in another form in a timeless sweet land.

Rumi

All for the love of you[13]

After our first night together, nothing changed with regards to how we interacted in front of others. By now people were used to us spending lots of time together, as everybody knew that I worked with him directly. So, it did not make a difference.

Whenever we were in the same location at the same time, I would join him alone or together with other men for dinner. He would never treat me in a reserved manner. His behaviour never spoke of a special effort to distance himself from me while with others in order to avoid any suspicions.

In fact – when in Taloqan and later in Khwaja Bahaudin - he sometimes encouraged me to have a "working breakfast" with him, too. I always thought this to be a clever way to show to the various people who would turn up in the morning with messages or requests that I was a stable fixture in his work.

On many occasions – whether in the Panjshir or Taloqan or Khwaja Bahaudin – there were often visits from his friends – his truly close circle, whose company he would seek more and more during the time we were together. These men became my friends as well. They accepted me as an equal – when with them it was not important that I was a woman, even though they would always treat me as a lady.

---

13 From the song "The Mystic's Dream" by Loreena McKinnett

Still – it cannot be emphasised often enough how unusual my position was and how lucky I was that my work there was not cut short by a "palace revolt". It must have been that they made a difference between me as a foreign woman who they probably considered to be "half a man" anyway. This allowed me certain freedoms and exceptions which would have never been granted to an Afghan woman.

Massoud and his friends would often read poems, new ones, classic ones, from local poets, Massoud Khalili's, his father's Khalilula Khalili, Hafiz, Rumi, translations from French and Italian classical poets, the list went on and on.

Taking pity on me they tried to translate them into French or English. Often, I did not quite understand, but that did not matter. He was with me, and we and his friends spent the most beautiful hours together. That was what mattered.

Poetry was Massoud's passion and even in the heat of battle, I was told, he would take out minutes at a time to read his beloved verses.

It all fitted his noblesse in mind and spirit: his love of horses and weapons, his passion for design and beauty. It was complimented by his strategic, sharp mind and his humanity and concern for mankind. His physical courage and tenacity were more obvious of his characteristics, while the former only opened to those close to him.

"He was a man, a real man" Fahim Dashty once lamented to me in 2006 when I sat in his Kabul Weekly office once more, like I had done many times before.

I once knocked on Massoud's door in Taloqan, as far as I remember it was May 2000, one evening, it was at round 10.00pm. When I did not hear a reply, I slowly opened the door and peeked through the gap. When I saw Massoud sit on the floor cushions and his friend Khalili sitting opposite him reciting a poem I gestured an apology and was about to close the door again, when Massoud called out my name and asked me not to be shy and to come in.

"Please come in – don't worry."

He wore a white Peraan Tombaan with a Western suit jacket over it. He sat with one leg pulled up to his chest, the other one bent on the floor, resting his right arm on one of the stuffed pillows. His hair was so beautiful, as always. Oh God, how he attracted me!

"I don't mean to disturb."

"You are never disturbing." He smiled at me "What is it?"

"I just wanted to let you know about some journalists' request to visit. I thought you might be alone, otherwise I would not have bothered you with this now."

"Don't worry about it. We can discuss this tomorrow, right – or do they need an answer straight away?"

"No, they didn't say so."

"Then join us, sit, please." He got up and walked to the back door calling for an aide to bring more tea. "The time we spend with our friends, hours like these are most important. The rest can wait." He sat down again.

"How are you, Ariana?" Khalili asked.

"I am very well. Sorry for interrupting you. Please continue I like to hear the melody of your poems – forgive me, even though I do not understand anything."

"Don't worry – this is not simple Persian – you have only just learned the common language."

I took the tray from the aide's hands and put it down in front of me.

We then continued listening to Khalili's poems. Both the men discussed them until midnight when Khalili got tired and excused himself.

When the door closed, I first kept on staring into the kerosene lamp with my chin resting on my knee, then looked at Massoud. God, what an attractive man he was!

Then I got up, let my chador slip to the back of my head, just barely stuck to some stubborn hair and sat next to him with my legs pulled towards my body.

"Those poems were beautiful, weren't they? I wish I could understand them."

"One day you will. And when I am old and grey and my eyesight is failing me, you will read them to me."

"Yes" I smiled at him.

"Do you know what just came to my mind?" I asked him after a couple of minutes of silence.

"No, tell me."

"I just remembered a song of a French singer I always liked a lot. Her name is Patricia Kaas and she has a song called "Je te dis vous"

"What does that mean – it doesn't seem to make any sense."

"You are right – but you will see when you hear the words. – I remembered this song because it is us – it is me. I will tell you the original lyrics first, then I will give you my version, o.k.?" I smiled at him.

He smiled back at me, with a body language that showed his full attention.

«Vous viviez comme un prince, je chantais pour trois sous

Dans un bal de province et je rêvais de vous

À la fin du polar, quand vous ne mouriez pas

Comme je l'enviais la dame qui souriait dans vos bras. »

Then I don't quite remember the lyrics, but it continues:

« C'était au mois de mai, j'm'en souviendrai toujours

J'étais morte d'angoisse, vous sachant la dans l'ombre

Puis sont venus vos fleurs et l'espoir d'un amour

Vous le grand, moi la p'tite, soyez là si je tombe

La gloire est si fragile mais bien moins que mon coeur

On dit qu'elle est le deuil éclatant du bonheur

À la fin du polar, si vous deviez mourir

J'essaierai c'est promis de garder le sourire

Et je te dis vous

M'avez éblouie

Moi qui n'étais rien

Vous qui saviez tout

Vous m'avez dit tu

Es belle, toute en noir

Quand vous êtes venu

M'écouter un soir »

So, the story of this song is: she is a singer, in love with this actor she has been admiring for many years, she says, she has been in love with him even be before they met. And when they finally meet, he actually falls in love with her, like she has dreamt, but is worried that all this is just a movie and that the love will die just like one of the heroes he has played ..."

"Yes."

"Now, I have re-worded this song:

« C'était au mois d'septembre, j'm'en souviendrai toujours
J'étais morte d'angoisse, vous rencontrer
Puis sont venus vos sourires et l'espoir d'un amour
Vous le grand, moi la p'tite, soyez là si je tombe
La gloire est si fragile mais bien moins que mon cœur
On dit qu'elle est le deuil éclatant du bonheur
À la fin de la guerre, si vous deviez mourir
J'essaierai c'est promis de garder le sourire
Et je te dis vous
M'avez éblouie
Moi qui n'étais rien
Vous qui saviez tout
Vous m'avez dit tu
Es belle, en salwar
Quand vous êtes venu
M'embrasser un soir » "

While I sang this song to him, he looked at me with a quiet little smile on his face. When I had finished, I paused.

"That is very sweet. And it is us, isn't it? But don't worry, this is not a film."

"No, just don't let me cry over you at the end of the war. Because I will not even try to make a promise to keep smiling.

You know that I thought of this song last year, too, when we were listening to music in the Astana, remember?"

"How can I forget – this is when I fell in love with you." He smiled and took my hand.

Then his face suddenly turned serious, and he looked at me for several seconds while I put my chin back onto my knee and stared once more into the kerosene lamp.

Then he bent over, removed my scarf from my neck, took the end of it and covered his nose in it.

"It smells like you" he said, smiling at me, affection pouring from his eyes. Then he unfolded the scarf, pulled me close and covered us both in it. I rested my head on his chest and wrapped my arms around his torso.

My God, how I am in love with him!

It was two in the morning when I left his house. For the whole day his scent would stay on my skin, his taste in my mouth, keeping me at an emotional high until we met again.

Given the fact that I had my tasks with numerous civilian projects and Massoud was pre-occupied with warfare we spent not more than fifty percent of our time in each other's company. So, whenever we had the chance to be truly alone – without being obvious – we would make the most of it. Sleep, then, seemed a waste of time and we often did not feel tired either.

On such occasions we talked about everything: everything that had moved us in that day, topics like politics, the current alliances, his people – the ones he trusted, the ones he did not trust, current affairs of the world – anything. We laughed a lot – at each other, with each other, about each other – we were often serious, we shared our emotions.

"Tell me what you love" he asked me once. We were sitting by ourselves in his house in Taloqan. It was already past midnight and must have been in February 1999 as I remember the snow in the streets, frost on the windows and the warm bukhari in the centre of his living room.

"I love YOU" I gave the obvious reply with a wink.

"I know" he smiled "Aside from that? Just say everything that comes to your mind"

"I love the Persian culture as it stretches and disseminates from Persia to North India – its colours, language, customs, music, faiths, its passionate spirit – most everything.

I love music, I love to dance.

I love Afghanistan, her people, her blue skies

I love the prayer call, I love the temples of India.

I love humble people with a big heart and great mind.

I love the French language, I love cheese, I love Italian food, I love animals – skiing, old things, coffee, Afghan chay, Indian Chay chocolate cake, honest and straight forward people, men who are men, yet cultured and open minded, commitment"

I paused

"What do you dislike – say everything."

"Ignorance, radicalism, stereotyping, many parts of the American culture, unsocial attitudes, profiteering, Jazz music, laziness, chauvinists, mismatched colours, sloppiness, dishonesty, misuse of trust, putting women second to men, evangelising in any religion."

He smiled at me and after a few seconds said, "You are like me – except for your love of coffee, chocolate cake and Italian food, which I did not have a chance to try, and your attraction to men's men – I would sign off with everything else."

I had to laugh, then I bent over and kissed him.

"No, seriously, I feel you and I think much alike ". He paused, looking at me with his intense eyes, calm face, and a little smile. "Talking to you comes so easy, I feel you understand me in what I am trying to say. You understand my feelings, worries, and hopes … It is amazing that someone born so far away from here could become so close to me.

And then - your kisses … I love your kisses; they are such a promise … "

"Of what?"

"A promise of your love to last for the rest of our live." he paused. "You will never have to tell me that you love me – I will know from the way you kiss me."

Massoud had a bad back, a problem with his spinal discs. At times he needed medical attention or just needed to rest for a couple of weeks at a time. He would then always retreat to his house in the Panjshir. Of course, he would never take the time out that it would have taken to better his condition – there was always too much which required his physical presence. Abdullah always became worried. As medical doctor he could always see that Massoud was not alright despite him claiming otherwise. "I can tell from the way he walks" he would always say.

On one such occasion in June 1999, he called me in Taloqan and asked me to stand in for him on final preparations and decisions regarding a school project in a village just south of Basarak. We had not seen each other for three weeks at that point.

This particular school was one of several being built. I oversaw all of them except for this one as it was not a girls' school.

For all other projects I was normally involved in, I was the one co-ordinating with the respective engineer and made sure the overall schedule was kept to. All details including sketches were all worked out and approved in co-operation with Massoud. I worked with the women, I made necessary purchases for equipment and others, if necessary, overseas.

So, I flew down to Panjshir.

Some sixty percent of my time, during these four years I would spend in the valley and would stay in the Astana guesthouse.

After J.B. left Afghanistan in November 1997, I remained in that same room which I had been assigned to. But after a while, after I had settled into my new life, I made it my own space. I asked them to remove the second bed and instead bring me floor cushions and stuffed pillows to have a nice sitting area. I laid out the room with carpets. Before that I had the room repainted in a subtle beige colour while before it was plain white. I had nice long curtains stitched by a tailor in Jangalak.

During my time in the Panjshir I would usually get up early to see the sunrise over the mountaintops from the large terrace the guesthouse featured and – when time permitted - I would stay out on that same terrace to see the sun set. During the cold season I enjoyed sitting on the windowsill in the lounge instead.

On my last afternoon before I was scheduled to go back to Taloqan I stood there just watching the world go by, reviewing my day, waiting for Massoud to go through the results of my meetings.

As I was leaning against the handrail, I heard the glass door open and Massoud walk across the terrace: "What is a pretty lady like you doing out here by herself?"

We exchanged a smile.

"How did things go today with the school?" he asked.

"It went well but there are still some issues they need to discuss among themselves" I replied. "But shouldn't you be resting?"

"Yes, I should and I have, but too many things are going on as usual".

"You know one issue which disturbs me is that they still do not have a conclusive plan on how to get all girls in the village to go to school. There are still families refusing to sign their daughters up. I was therefore thinking that perhaps someone from our side could speak to the men of the shura there, explaining to them again how important it is to get a basic education for their daughters."

"Yes, absolutely – I will look into this.

Was there anything else? Did the men co-operate with you?"

"Oh yes. They know that I am acting on your behalf, so there is total respect. I had no problems.

But there are several details regarding the construction of the school itself. Shall we go inside and talk about this?"

"Sure"

We walked together across the terrace towards the glass door which led into the corridor of the guesthouse. He opened the door for me. As we stepped in, we left our shoes outside as it is custom in every Afghan house.

We then went to the lounge to go through all these points for the next one hour, me pulling out several documents, highlighting to Massoud the relevant issues.

Whenever we worked together like that, we were not lovers we were partners in the common task of building the areas under our control. We were not man and woman we were co-workers drawing on each other's experience and opinions. We would normally be serious, and I would follow his lead as his was usually the right way – sensible and thought through. How much I learned from him in technical aspects as well as soft skills! He taught me most of what I am today – leadership, humanity, poetry, technicalities of buildings and structures, Islam, and Sufism. But that did not mean that he dominated me. By contrast we exchanged a lot of opinions, views, and knowledge – and we moulded all that into what became "us". He loved me for what I was, for my believes and thoughts, for the emotions I drew from his heart.

"So, I believe the construction is going to take longer than planned. If we are lucky, we can finish before the cold weather sets in."

"That is alright – I prefer there to be consensus among everybody about what is required rather than rushing the job. So, thanks for doing this so efficiently for me."

"You know that I will do everything for you, don't you?"

"I know" he smiled at me and then let his eyes wander out of the window towards the mountains. I looked at his profile from the side. He just had incredibly aquiline features. And his eyes, his eyes! Whenever he spoke to somebody he would look straight at the person with his full attention, processing every word.   At the same time, I observed repeatedly that when he was uncomfortable with somebody for this or the other reason, he would avoid that person's eyes. Still smiling he would move on, giving himself an air of arrogance.

"Do you want to meet in your room in a few minutes?" he asked after a pause

My heart skipped a beat – did I want to??

"Sure." I smiled at him and got up to leave, picking up my folder. I walked to my room and in the remaining time I brushed my teeth, closed the drapes, brushed my hair, put on some perfume and tried to calm my anticipation. I was the only "guest" here at the moment, so Massoud had to be careful not to be seen entering my room by one of the caretakers.

When he knocked on my door I was already on fire – several minutes can be so long!

When he entered, he took off his pakul and slowly walked towards me, then just held me for a few seconds.

He was wearing a Piraan Tombaan with a vest over it. I loved it when he wore traditional clothes. He looked very dignified in them, especially with his hair starting to turn grey. He kissed my forehead and then asked in a soft voice:

"How are you, my darling? Are you coping? Is anybody giving you a hard time?"

"I am fine – don't worry about me. I am getting along with everybody just fine. Especially Abdullah is a gem. If there were problems, I would let you know."

I did get along fine with everybody I was involved with. Slowly but surely the men had understood that I supported them one hundred percent, that my heart and soul was here and of course they realised that I had Massoud's full confidence. So little by little I could expand my authority proofing to them over and over again that I could be trusted, that – despite being a woman, despite being a foreigner – I was to be taken seriously, or else.

It was very important to follow their customs, follow their style which I enjoyed. Even towards foreigners I behaved like an Afghan woman – of course never wearing the Chadori, but never shaking hands and so forth. Only when Massoud and I were alone with a Westerner would I turn more open as I knew Massoud liked me that way. He liked my style when we were alone, he liked my frankness, he liked my openness and straight forward thinking. At the same time, he appreciated that I did not act on all this in public as he just was too aware of the limitations the Afghan society imposed on women and their credibility.

"Good … good."

"I have been missing you."

"Why do you think I am here?"

I smiled at him and stroked his cheek.

With that he gently pushed me against the wall, tilted his head and started kissing me.

It was such a contrast. When he was taking his day-to-day decisions, he did everything fast – he thought fast, he acted fast, he walked fast. Mostly he was far ahead of his commanders and sometimes did not seem to know whether to explain his thoughts to them or simply give them orders. Because of that he sometimes appeared harsh with his men, but at the end of the day was always a benevolent leader, never dominating people unreasonably. His men trusted and followed him because they knew that his judgement and orders were the right ones.

From young he must have been used to being ahead of the pack – intellectually, physically. He had an intensity about him, which I found exhilarating. I loved to watch him take decisions and get on with things. He was hard to challenge in an argument, he would have thought it through before most his opponents got around to it. To some people however, that was too fast a pace, and some were intimidated.

But when it came to tenderness, he was in no rush.

"Why do you love me?" he asked after a while lying on my bed on his back, looking at the ceiling "I have nothing to offer you and you have to share my attention."

"You have everything I want and more" I replied "I have learned so much from you. I do not only love you, but I admire you deeply for your mind and heart, your courage and all that you are."

He then turned to me and put his left arm around my waist, I turned in the same direction with my back towards him. We just lay like that for some ten or fifteen minutes without saying a word. With the drapes drawn and the sun setting, my room was painted in a soft light. I looked at the simple wood furniture, the blankets, the carpets, and the windows with their white frames leading out onto the terrace which peaked out from behind the drapes.

I took his hand which was resting on my hip and folded my fingers around his. There was no luxury here, yet I had never been so happy.

"Tomorrow I don't want you to go back just yet" he said after a while as he sat up, kissed my shoulder, and got up. "My closest friends, my closest circle is meeting tomorrow. You know them all, they all know you. We are meeting at my house. There is a certain matter to discuss, and I want you to be a part of that."

I was surprised, to say the least.

But I trusted him of course – not so much for my sake, but that he had covered his own back.

When I got to his house the next morning at eight o'clock Abdullah was already there. We sat down outside where they had prepared a group of chairs, tea was already on the table.

"Salamaleikum, khub hastyn" he greeted me, shaking my hand.

"Waleikum, Doctor Sahib, khub hastyn - shukur" I replied with the usual pleasantry.

"You have been busy, haven't you?" Abdullah began the conversation in English.

"Yah, quite" I replied "but as you know we don't feel the strain, do we? You just ramble on; after all there are only twenty-four hours in one day ..." I smiled at him.

"Absolutely. But sometimes you look at the bigger picture and your heart sinks. Look at what's going on around us. Will we ever make it? I worry more and more that we may be in our last season hunting."

"It will be hard. No doubt. But I have full confidence that we will be the winners in the end. We can sit this out. My gut tells me this. And Amir Sahib believes that, too."

"Yes, I know. Let's hope that you all are right ...

On a different subject, can I tell you something before we start?"

"Yes of course."

"You know, you have to understand that I know about the relationship that you and Amir Sahib are having." He paused for a second, then added quickly:

"And, please believe me, I have no problems with that. You both are too alike to not fall in love, and I wish from the bottom of my heart that this will never cause any problems. He needs you – you offer him things his wife can't give him. You can match up with him intellectually and at the same time give him the thrills of an attractive woman - and that he has never experienced. You know he is a dedicated father and all – but he is a man, too, and I could see from the beginning that you overwhelmed him. I noticed early in the day how he looked at you, how he spoke to you; at first, I saw danger on the horizon. But then things seemed to go well."

He paused, looking at me with his typical concerned expression hoping to see a sign from me which showed that I understood what he was saying.

"I appreciate you understanding this."

"So anyway, you should be aware that he is running quite a big risk of bringing you here today. You will find that only his most trusted circle will be here, nobody else he can't trust 150%. That he wants you to be part of his decision-making body is a huge step and you should know that this proofs everything to you."

"Thank you for being such a good friend. I really appreciate you telling me that. And I will remember it always. I just hope I can justify his decision."

"You can – I know. As far as I am concerned you are the best thing that ever happened to him. And he must know it, too. Otherwise, you would not be here.

He is, despite him being such a tough and enduring man, very sensitive and honest. He will walk through fire for his friends but if you disappoint him that will hurt him deeply."

"I will rather die but disappoint him. In fact, I want to die with him, when it's his time – I could not survive without him anyway.

You know, I have never loved like this before. I know that, strictly speaking, it is not right what we are doing but it is too strong and beautiful to ignore – we can't.

He tried; you know. At first, he tried not to give in to his feelings. But in the end, it was him who opened the doors for us. I never seduced him, you know. Just once, when the moment was right, I made it clear to him how I feel, and he told me that he felt the same but said he could not do this. After a week, Abdullah, he could not stand it anymore and that's when it all began."

"I understand all that – don't worry – no trouble will come from my side."

I smiled at him, then lowered my eyes.

"Tell me something: how is his wife? I know that she is my age – but one thing I have been wondering; how can a man like Amir Sahib be satisfied with a comparatively simple woman like that?"

"See that is the point." Abdullah replied "I, like all of his friends, I do not know her well, she is a traditional woman, she will not mix with the men. I know that he loves her, but more so his children – you know that he adores them. But, and you are right there, he is missing the intellectual kick-back. Before he met you, I'm sure he wasn't even aware that he has been longing for a woman-companion, because this concept does not exist here. Someone like you who truly loves what he loves, an Afghan at heart, like you who shares his values – moderate as they are – who fights alongside him and supports him. At the same time, he is a man, as I said, if you know what I mean?"

I nodded and smiled.

"I am sorry, I did not mean to be rude ..."

"No, no, you are not – you are my brother. And I am so glad about your words."

He smiled.

"Such a companionship which he found in you is not ever found in Afghanistan. Men and women are not friends in that sense. They are, well, men and women and most men here have very limited ideas as to what role they want their women to play in their life.

You see, Amir Sahib has no choice but to except his wife the way she is – to match up with a man in general or with him in particular, you must come from a different background. If you are from a traditional background, there is no way that you will have the confidence to do what you are doing. But he is attracted by that. He, at heart, does not want a traditional woman, but he does not want a purely Western one either, that I know because he does not share their values.

So, anyway, that is the reason why he is overwhelmed by you. That is why he could not bear to be 'reasonable' and that is why he wants you to be here today."

A few minutes later Massoud came walking in with his fragile yet manly frame and typical determined steps, prayer beads in hand, Marshal Fahim and Yunus Qanuni in his trail. He looked at me with a smile and then turned to Abdullah.

"Where is the rest?"

"They should be here soon"

I greeted the men one by one exchanging a few polite words.

At that moment in time a lot of new developments had occurred with regards to relationship between the US and the United Front.

By 1999, Massoud was seen by some at the Pentagon and inside the Clinton Cabinet as a spent force commanding a band of thugs. An inner circle of the US cabinet was sharply divided over whether the United States should deepen its partnership with him. Secretary of State Madeleine Albright and the chairman of the Joint Chiefs of Staff, Henry Shelton - reflecting the views of professional analysts in their departments - argued that Massoud's alliance was tainted and in decline.

But at the CIA, especially inside the Counterterrorist Center, career officers passionately described Massoud by 1999 as the United States' last, best hope to capture or kill bin Laden in Afghanistan before his al Qaeda network claimed more American lives. Massoud might be a flawed ally, they declared, but bin Laden was by far the greater danger. Massoud had of course acquired that image during the Kabul disaster where he was unable to avoid having the crimes committed by his allies spill over onto his reputation.

Frightened by swelling intelligence reports warning that al Qaeda planned new terrorist strikes, President Bill Clinton's national security adviser, Samuel R. Berger, and his counterterrorism director, Richard Clarke, approved what they code-named, the "JAWBREAKER-5" mission. This was the plan to send a team of CIA officers to meet Massoud and discuss possibilities of co-operation. They were uneasy about Massoud but said they were ready to try anything within reason that might lead to Bin Laden's capture or death.

It was for this newly arisen US interest in the United Front that our meeting that June 1999 took place.

As it was his style, Massoud wasted no time to come to the point.

"As some of you already know, we have been approached by the American CIA for a renewed co-operation. However, these approaches have been vague and with no concrete proposals. They want to send a small team of their agents here to discuss ways forward. The way I see it, the US is mainly worried about the rise of Al Quaida and Osama rather than rescuing Afghanistan from further decline."

Massoud had a long and chequered history with the CIA. The CIA had first sent Massoud aid in 1984. But their relations were undermined by the CIA's heavy dependence on Pakistan during the war against the Soviets. The Pakistani intelligence service despised Massoud because he had waged a long and brutal campaign against Pakistan's main Islamic radical client, the warlord Gulbuddin Hekmatyar. As the war against the Soviets ended, Pakistani intelligence sought to exclude Massoud from the victory, and the CIA mainly went along. But under pressure from the State Department and members of Congress, the agency eventually reopened its private channels to Massoud.

134

In 1990 the CIA's secret relationship with Massoud soured because of a dispute over a $500,000 payment. Gary Schroen, a CIA officer then working from Islamabad, Pakistan, had delivered the cash to Massoud's brother in exchange for assurances that Massoud would attack Afghan communist forces along a key artery, the Salang Highway. But Massoud's forces never moved, so far as the CIA could tell. Schroen and other officers believed they had been ripped off for half a million dollars. But Massoud had always maintained that he never received the money.

Since 1996, however the CIA had made shy attempts to renew the contact with him.

Garry Schroen, who had facilitated the previous monetary transactions renewed contact with Massoud during a solo visit to Kabul in September 1996. By then bin Laden had found sanctuary in Afghanistan, and the CIA sought allies to watch and disrupt Al Qaeda. Schroen and Massoud settled their old dispute. Massoud then agreed to cooperate on a secret CIA program to repurchase Stinger anti-aircraft missiles. He sold the agency eight missiles he still possessed and began to talk sporadically with Langley about intelligence operations against bin Laden.

Schroen had met with Massoud again in the spring of 1997 in Taloqan. By then, the Taliban had stormed into Kabul and seized the capital as our forces withdrew. Looking to win American favour for his prolonged war against the Taliban and its foreign Islamic militant allies, Massoud began to buy up Stingers across the north for the CIA. He also agreed to notify the agency if he got a line on bin Laden's whereabouts.

A series of clandestine CIA teams carrying electronic intercept equipment and relatively small amounts of cash -- up to $250,000 each time - began to visit Massoud in the Panjshir Valley. The first formal group, code-named NALT-1, flew on one of our helicopters from Dushanbe to the Panjshir Valley late in 1997. Each team carried cash of up to US$250,000

Three other teams would go in by June 1999. The electronic intercept equipment they delivered allowed us to monitor Taliban battlefield radio transmissions. In exchange the CIA officers asked Massoud to let them know immediately if his men ever heard accounts on the Taliban radios indicating that bin Laden or his top lieutenants were on the move in a particular sector.

However, given the doubts about Massoud inside the Clinton administration, the CIA's push to deepen its partnership with him faced close scrutiny at the White House. The National Security Council's intelligence policy and legal offices drafted formal, binding guidelines.

"Also," Abdullah added "the problem is that they are only concentrating on Osama rather than seeing the complete problem we and the region are facing. Osama is a part of the problem but not the problem itself.

Ariana, do you remember that last meeting we had with the Jawbreaker team a couple weeks ago?" He turned to me "it became so clear that their mission is still defined in a very narrow manner, didn't it?"

"Yes," I said "they are sitting on the fence and that's a dangerous situation for us because we do not know what support will come from their side at the end of it all. If we give them detailed intelligence about Osama, they will take it and after that nothing else will come from them. We should tie in our information supply with concrete demands for weapon supplies."

I had indeed attended this meeting with the CIA agents. I served as the interpreter to Massoud.

The team of five agents were visibly shocked to see me and almost ended up talking to me exclusively for the first half hour, bombarding me with all sorts of questions. When Massoud introduced us, I noticed with joy that he was proud to show me off to the Americans. When I spoke to them, I could see he was looking at me all the time. He did not speak English, so he did not understand a word of what I was talking to them, so Abdullah translated for him and his face spoke of pride that I worked for him.

"Agreed" Massoud said, the typical four lines carving his forehead "but we should also not push it too far otherwise the whole situation may turn on us. We have already received valuable amounts of money. What I mean is we have nothing to lose. Whatever bit we are getting from them will help us."

"And of course, chances are that via these operations the US may soon understand Afghanistan's plight and will be encouraged to help us on a grander scale." I nodded

"That's another plus point – I see it that way, too." He looked at me, then letting his eyes circle the round:

"So do you all agree with me that we have nothing to lose in co-operating with the Americans for the moment?"

Everybody nodded.

So, from here onward a cooperation of limited scope carried on.

Other meetings with commanders and other people of his close circle often took place in Dr Abdullah's house, in the small village of Dashtak.

Some 20 minutes' drive from Jangalak towards the southern entrance of the valley, the house is rather grand with a beautiful rose garden. Abdullah's sister lived here with her family as well.

The house has several guest and lounge rooms, with one spectacular pavilion laid out with floor cushions overlooking the river. In the early nineties Massoud himself designed an extension to the living room of the main house.

Here we would sometimes have hour-long discussions about political issues.

It was once in September 1999 when we spent a Friday afternoon at that house. I arrived with Massoud and several of his relatives after they had attended Friday prayers at the nearby small mosque. I always enjoyed arriving with him, with his close circle, I enjoyed being part of that.

We first sat in the garden for two hours with casual conversation, simply relaxing on this beautiful Juma[14].

Nobody bothered with me being the only woman in the circle, as usual, just part of the conversation, part of the scene. Only the servants of the house would always look at me in astonishment. They would look at my face and clothes, not quite knowing where to place me – even after seeing me several times. But the men had not bothered for a long time

So, we sat under the blue Afghan sky, under the large trees of the garden, which was overlooking the river. Yet again the discussion soon turned to political issues.

---

[14] Friday, day of special prayers in the Muslim faith

After a while I got up to sit on the wall, securing the property by the river. This wall drops down sharply into the flowing waters. I took off my shoes and let my feet dangle down. The noise of the water rushing over a power-generating water wheel nearby is quite loud. That is why I did not hear Massoud approach after some thirty minutes to squat down next to me

"I much enjoy this place every time we come here," he began as he, too, took off his shoes. "I want to own a garden like that myself one day."

"Peace will come, and you will own your house and garden".

A pause.

"Amir Sahib" a servant approached us from behind "dinner is ready."

We got up and made our way back to the table under the trees. They had served the food already.

"Get up – look at this perfect weather. I want to walk with you along the river before breakfast". The following morning Massoud had knocked on my window, standing outside the pavilion which overlooks the river. This space had been reserved for me to sleep in – at least one perk of being a woman in such circumstances.

"Sure – Give me five minutes. I see you in the back".

He turned around and started walking towards the far end of the property.

A few minutes later we stepped out of the gate at the rear end of the estate, took a sharp right and walked past the village mosque to the river.

The bank was full of pebbles, large ones, and small ones so we only walked very slowly. After a while we squatted down, right next to the water's edge, some two hundred metres from the village.

"The big trees over there" Massoud pointed towards the mosque "were bombed by the Russians in an effort to take our shelter away. But now see into what they have grown again. Big and strong trees.

I wish this were an analogy for Afghanistan."

"Oh, I firmly believe in that. The Afghans are a resilient bunch, just like those trees. But what is needed in this country is a strong leadership, a benevolent one. Then the country can be re-built."

"Yes, you are right. One of the biggest mistakes we made in Kabul was to distribute power among too many people. Someone should have taken charge, someone with the country at heart"

"You should have been that someone"

"No, my darling, I could not manage to control my people, too much blood was wasted."

"Next time, you will have learned from all that and you will know what to do. And I will be there to help you." I looked at him.

"Yes, I much would like you to do that for me. Insh Allah this day is not far off."

Snow on the Sahara[15]

Doing everything for the one you love, trying to make the impossible possible, to sooth the other's pain even by conjuring up snow in the burning desert.

By 1999 this had become my life's mission, my obsession at times. I tried to ease his workload wherever I could and be there for him when exhaustion and doubts overcame him - I tried to cool the desert.

All considered I spent more time with him than his wife – even though we were often separated. As time moved on and people got used to my presence, I went with him almost everywhere except into battle activities. I even accompanied him on his trips abroad.

For example, it was in December 1999 when we took a trip to Moscow. This trip was actually designed to be carried out by Massoud alone and meant to get military support from Moscow. We had maintained constant diplomatic representation with Russia since 1995 and these were to pay off now in times of desperate need.

Both our relations to Russia as well as to Iran were a double-edged sword, however, as this was one of the reasons cited why the US government looked at Massoud with suspicion and was unwilling to give not more than the absolutely necessary to get some commitment from us to help in the search for bin Laden.

---

[15] Song by Angun

And nothing came for free from Iran and Russia either. All weapon supplies had to be bought – at a small discount – but no donations.

It was for that reason that Massoud undertook that one-day trip. He was supposed to meet our ambassador and his military attaché.

This trip was kept highly confidential and even I had no idea until Massoud came to see me in my house in Taloqan at two in the afternoon on December 13th, a crisp and bright day.

When he knocked, I opened the door, as always happy to see him. "Salam, ma chère." He smiled at me and pushed the door close behind him. "Nice and toasty in here."

"Yes, you know me, I need it warm ...".

"Do you want to come with me to Moscow?" he asked then without warning, walking towards my floor cushions behind the bukhari and sat down.

"Where? Moscow? Well, yes, of course. When?"

"This afternoon before sun-down"

"What?"

"Yes – this has been planned for a while now. Highly confidential – I want nobody to know about this, but I'd like you to be with me. "

I smiled at him. "Of course, I come with you"

"We will meet Ahmad Zia there – remember? He is our military attaché, Abdullah's nephew?"

"Oh yes – I remember – he likes to smoke a lot."

"Oh, you also observed that? He tries his best to hide this habit, though."

"Yes, but not successfully to the keen observer" I laughed, sitting down next to him.

He stroked my cheek.

"I will pray now – why don't you take lunch in the meantime?"

At 4pm we boarded the helicopter heading for Dushanbe.

We arrived in Moscow at one o'clock in the morning, received only by Ahmad Zia. Snow was falling as we drove to town in one of the embassy cars. Ahmad expressed his surprise that Massoud had travelled almost alone.

"Why make a big fuzz? More people will not help this situation. We are better off on a very small scale."

"Yes" Ahmad smiled, instructing the driver to go straight to the ambassador's residence where several Russian government officials were waiting for us.

"Can we go to your house first?" Massoud turned to Ahmad "I want to pray before the meeting"

Given the advanced time Ahmad looked concerned but did not dare say anything it appeared to me. Once at his house Massoud inquired about the direction to Mekka and Ahmad pointed accordingly.

"Are you sure?" Massoud teased him "I know you don't pray so I don't trust you knowing these things; you know it will be your responsibility if God does not accept my prayers this time" he teased and laughed

It was three o'clock in the morning when we finally met with the Russian government officials.

25th December 1999

When I got up in the morning, as in the previous two years, I found a candle on my desk in Panjshir with a note in Massoud's handwriting reading "Merry Christmas", in English. And in Dari: blessings of Isa[16] on this day. – I never received more meaningful Christmas gifts!

By that time in December 1999, I had grown well into my work and responsibilities. It had been two years since the whirlwind of events had deposited me here.

On top of my civilian projects and the media work, during military activities, while Massoud was with his troops at the front, I would always be part of the administrative and organisational back-up in Taloqan as well as Khwajah Bahauddin or even Basarak or Jabal o Seraj in the Shomali Plain, often shuttling back and forth between these places.

Massoud had one jeep and a driver assigned to me. The driver's name was Ahmad, too, Ahmad Jalali; an extremely loyal man, he would have given his life for "the boss" at any given moment. Whenever he was driving me, I sitting in the backseat as expected of a woman, he would tell me about his family. He was from Istalif. While the village was part of the Northern Alliance territory he and his family would stay there. After this artisan village was destroyed in 1999 by the Taliban, he shifted his family to the Valley. When Istalif was liberated and Massoud ordered the reconstruction he had come to downright worship his "Amir Sahib".

---

[16] Isa is the Arabic name for Jesus, as per the Quran

I would work the phone, I would do whatever I could and whatever was socially permissible to me as a foreign woman to help the present offensive, I would do whatever it took. When we had to evacuate Taloqan, for example it was largely my responsibility to ensure that all women and children were taken care of, and the withdrawal did not impact their lives above and beyond what was necessary.

I was known in most of the villages and the surrounding areas, I visited the women of many families on a regular basis, became friends with them. That way it was easier to align our actions with the concerns of the people there and on the other hand make them understand what was going on in Afghanistan and what we were all trying to achieve in this or the other instant.

As already in the Panjshir I was not only assisting Massoud with whatever he asked me to do and Abdullah with media and foreign relations, but I also made it a personal point to get involved with the women of the villages and tried to make a difference in their lives.

I tried to assess their conditions, their problems and then propose to Massoud measures to better their situations. If not too much expenditure was involved – which we simply could not afford as military considerations always took prevalence – I had free hand in these things.

There was for example Sajya, 20 years old living in a small house in Taloqan together with her two brothers and her in-laws, the husband a sheep farmer.

When I met her in May 1999, she was pregnant with her third child. She had given birth twice before, but the unlucky girl lost both babies: the first was still born, the second died after two months from tuberculosis. With a lack of doctors and medicine the boy stood no chance.

145

Now she was under pressure from her in-laws to finally produce a healthy child – preferably of course a boy.

Then there was Saima who lived in a small mud hut in the corner of a mud compound owned by her father-in-law in the Shomali Plain, not far from the village of Istalif.

Two years ago, her husband Hanif had been killed by the Taleban. He was a mujahideen. She had been engaged when she was 15 years old.

He left her with her three sons, Shakir, seven, Nusrat, four and Zakir, three, and no way of supporting herself. She had no money and no way of making money.

She first made a basic living by serving other people in the village. She would get a loaf of bread or some food as payment. She would work on farms and in houses doing anything.

To enable her to make a living we gave her a cow so that she could make a living by milking the cow and selling the milk and yoghurt. That way she could make some money and still work as a domestic for other people to get food and basics to help her live from day-to-day.

The cow did not cost us much, yet it changed the live of that family dramatically.

Ever since, she would wave from far when I came to visit her. She had changed into a proud woman, no longer dependant on people. It was a joy to see. Still the family was very poor but at least they did not have to worry for their bread tomorrow.

Then there was Anisgul, a fifty-year-old woman in Khwaja Bahaudin. While she and her family were not doing too badly, her husband was a heroin addict, a problem many men dealt

146

with in the northern parts of Afghanistan where the poppy cultivation still supplied large parts of Europe and America with heroin. Some of the producers themselves became addicts. In all areas directly controlled by Massoud all poppy cultivation was strictly forbidden and Massoud saw to it that it was enforced. In other areas not under his direct control but governed by his allies of the United Front poppy cultivation has remained a problem throughout, not least because some of the commanders were addicts themselves.

Overall, it was medical problems which needed addressing in our areas. The second layer of problems to be unravelled were of social nature – something much harder to address and to introduce betterment.

The medical issues needed funds, which the United Front – or what was left of it at times – lacked for their own effort. So, my main partners were international NGOs which had not given up on Afghanistan and their brave staff who ventured into the even remotest areas to help ease the suffering of the people. I mainly hooked up with Medicains Sans Frontieres and the International Red Cross.

Whenever I met someone with a persistent medical problem, I would try to organise transport to the closest doctor, which often was several hours drive away. I sometimes felt guilty. When I needed medical attention, the Tajik hospitals were only a one-hour flight away. But for these people?

There were also doctors who had stayed on in Afghanistan or had returned despite or because this still being a war zone.

One of those brave examples was Dr Hajirah Zia Bahrustani. She ran a maternity hospital in Badakhshan. After an eight-hour day there she saw patients in her private little clinic in her home village. This remotest of provinces had been spared the rule of the Taliban but was also the poorest.

There was – and to my knowledge still is - only one maternity hospital in Badakhshan. The hospital had just 20 beds.

The lack of health care was and still is one of the main reasons why, in this region, almost one in 10 mothers die in childbirth – the highest recorded rate of maternal mortality in the world. Lack of electricity makes it impossible to get sterilisation units up and running. Water from a nearby river has to be collected in buckets and boiled on firewood.

We had become aware of this Badakhshan hospital via a letter Dr. Bahrustani wrote to Massoud urging him to help in their lifesaving efforts.

This appeal prompted me to travel there myself to have a look at the place. Massoud sent me there by helicopter. He had taken out 50,000 "Rupees"[17] for me to bring along. After half an hour's flight I touched down in an open field near the hospital itself. Dr. Bahrustani welcomed me personally. She spoke fluent English, so we communicated very well.

We sat down for tea for about an hour to get acquainted. Then she showed me around the hospital, explained a few cases of patients to me. While the place was kept in reasonable general hygienic condition, it could not cope by far with the hygiene standards a delivering mother required. The need was obvious and when I presented her with the money, she was close to tears.

"This was personally authorised by Amir Sahib to help out a bit. We hope it can make a difference. We would love to help more and give good healthcare for the whole of Afghanistan. But you know what dire straits we are in as a militia force ourselves. We have barely enough to stand up against the Taliban. No substantial assistance which would enable us to

---

[17] A colloquial expression for Afghani, not to be confused with the Indian rupee.

sweep the Talib menace out of this country is coming from the Western powers, so we are also very cash strapped. Whatever is available will go into the Panjshir first of course – this is our home ground, you must understand. All our reciprocated loyalties are there."

"You do not know what difference this money will make here. We thank you so very much. May Allah bless you and Amir Sahib and all our brave fighters."

As the months went on, especially from late 1999 onward, it appeared to me that Massoud turned more and more weary of his life of seemingly never-ending strive and more and more often we talked for hours of the political situation and discussed options. We talked much about our faiths, about his vision for Afghanistan.

It more and more poured out of him – his dreams his longings. And I shared them all – what he felt, what he hoped, I felt and hoped the same. I did not have to try. I was in pain when he was. I felt for this country just like him. She had grown so close to my heart – her landscapes, her people, her culture, language, and customs. And of course, it was all connected to him, to his vision for this country, to his ideals which I shared just the same.

Whenever he spoke to a journalist about these things he said: " 'we' believe in ..." insinuating that all his people believed in the equality of women, a democratic system etc. But on such occasions, I always thought to myself: no, my darling, it is you, who believes in all of this, and your people follow this for now because you have proven to be their effective leader. If left to their own devices, none of them would have this clear vision and most would muddle the message with traditional thinking which would not bring a clear structure to this country.

By this time, he had gotten very disillusioned with the Western powers. How often had he appealed to the US government for help? How often had he highlighted the Pakistani connections to the world? Had anybody really listened, much less bothered? He felt that he shared many of the West's ideals such as freedom, self-determination, women's rights, and democracy, but he felt increasingly let down.

What had mainly caused this disillusionment was the way the sudden American rapprochement ended or rather by far not delivered on the potential prospected.

In October of the previous year Massoud had last met with the Jawbreaker team in the Panjshir. He wanted me and Abdullah to be part of these meetings yet again.

Massoud told the CIA team that he was willing to deepen his partnership with the CIA, but he was explicit about his limitations. Bin Laden spent most of his time near the southern city of Kandahar, in the eastern Afghan mountains, far from where Massoud's forces operated. Occasionally bin Laden visited Jalalabad or Kabul, closer to the Northern Alliance's lines. In these areas Massoud's intelligence service had active agents, and perhaps they could develop more sources.

Massoud also told the CIA delegation that U.S. policy toward bin Laden and Afghanistan was doomed to fail. The Americans directed all their efforts against bin Laden and a handful of his senior aides, but they failed to see the larger context in which al Qaeda thrived. What about the Taliban? What about the Taliban's supporters in Pakistani intelligence? What about its financiers in Saudi Arabia and the United Arab Emirates?

"Even if we succeed in what you are asking for," Massoud told the CIA delegation "that will not solve the bigger problem that is growing."

The CIA officers told Massoud they agreed with his critique, but they had their orders. The U.S. government rejected a military confrontation with the Taliban or direct support for any armed factions in the broader Afghan war. Instead, U.S. policy focused on capturing bin Laden and his lieutenants for criminal trial or killing them during an arrest attempt. If Massoud helped with this narrow mission, the CIA officers argued, perhaps it would lead to wider political support or development aid in the future. But in the meantime, their hands were bound.

Despite these odds, during 2000 Massoud planned an expanding military campaign against the Taliban and al Qaeda. His strategy was to recruit allies such as Ismail Khan and Abdul Rashid Dostum and seed them as pockets of rebellion against Taliban rule in northern and western Afghanistan, where the Taliban was weakest. As these rebel pockets emerged and stabilized, he would drive toward them with his more formal armoured militia, trying to link up on roadways, choking off Taliban-ruled cities and towns.

Once he had more solid footing in the north, Massoud planned to pursue the same strategy in the Taliban heartland in the south. He hoped to aid ethnic Pashtun rebels such as Hamid Karzai, a former Afghan deputy foreign minister from a prominent royal tribal family who had been forced into exile in Pakistan. By 1999, after the murder of his father by Taliban, Hamid Karzai had turned against them and wanted to lead a rebellion in their southern homeland around Kandahar. Massoud dispatched aides to meet with Karzai and develop these ideas.

In private talks in person and by satellite telephone, Karzai told Massoud he was ready to slip inside Afghanistan and fight. "Don't move into Kandahar," Massoud told him during a phone conversation I witnessed. "You must go to a place where you can hold your base." In that same phone call Massoud invited Karzai to the north. Subsequently Karzai met with Massoud on several occasions. Almost five years younger than him he soon brimmed with reverence towards Massoud.

I only met Hamid Karzai once, in early 2000 when he came to Khwaja Bahaudin. I was introduced to him over dinner, but never had any official dealings with him. When he was explained who I was and what I was doing here he expressed his admiration in his typical, straight forward – sometimes overly simplistic – way. He left the impression on me that he was friendly at heart, but perhaps not the deepest puddle you might encounter. And of course, he too, was no match for Massoud. The man I love had no match: he was polite, he was intelligent, funny, and attractive in mind, body and soul. When I looked at him on such occasions, following his beautiful, deep eyes, I was flushed with such love and affection that I had to smile to myself.

To pursue his plans of linking the pocket of resistance throughout the country in a serious way, we needed helicopters, trucks, and other vehicles. Some CIA officers wanted to help us by supplying the mobile equipment, cash, training, and weapons we would need to expand his war against the Taliban and al Qaeda. Yet as 2000 passed, the CIA struggled to maintain the basics of its intelligence liaison with us.

It was difficult and risky for the agency's officers to reach the Panjshir Valley. The only practical route was through Tajikistan. From there CIA teams usually took one of the few rusting, patched-together Mi-17 transport helicopters our people managed to keep in the air. On one trip, the Taliban scrambled MiG-21 jets in an effort to shoot down Massoud's helicopter but failed.

Even on the best days, the choppers would shake, and rattle and the cabin would fill with the smell of fuel. The overland routes were no better. When a CIA team drove in from Dushanbe one day, one of its vehicles flipped over and an officer dislocated his shoulder.

These reports accumulated on the desk of Deputy Director of Operations James Pavitt, who had overall responsibility for CIA espionage. Pavitt was a former station chief who had served in Europe during the Cold War.

Pavitt began to ask why CIA officers were taking such huge physical risks to work with Massoud. And the question asked repeatedly in Washington was whether they were getting enough to justify the possibility of death or injury?

Those opposed to the Panjshir missions argued "You're sending people to their deaths."

The agency eventually sent out a team of mechanics knowledgeable about Russian helicopters. But not knowledgeable enough, in fact, because when our men opened one of the Mi-17s, they were stunned: The mechanics had patched an engine originally made for a Hind attack helicopter into the bay of the Mi-17. It was a flying miracle!

Afterward Tenet signed off on a compromise: The CIA would buy its own airworthy Mi-17 helicopter, maintain it properly in Tashkent, Uzbekistan, and use CIA pilots to fly clandestine teams into the Panjshir.

But the helicopter issue was a symptom of a larger problem. As mentioned above by the late summer of 2000, the CIA's liaison with us was fraying.

Frustrated by daunting geography and unable to win support for Massoud in US cabinet debates, the CIA's officers felt stifled.

For our part we had hoped our work with the agency would lead to clearer recognition of Afghanistan's plight in Washington and perhaps covert military aid, not to mention a solution to the Pakistan problem. But we could see no evidence that this was happening. Instead, we were badgered repeatedly about capturing Bin Laden alive. The limited scope of the US involvement continued right into 2001.

We began to wonder more and more whether the US had a plan to begin with – particularly after a successful capture of Bin Laden. My personal view was: not.

I pointed out to Massoud that in other parts of the world, too, the US had been sitting on the fence. After Vietnam where they clearly stuck out there head too far and received the setback of their recent history, they had been reluctant to support "rebel" movements in proxy countries.

"They might not do it openly and directly anymore but supporting the Taliban indirectly is at least as bad, isn't it?" Massoud replied.

"Absolutely. See – the problem with the Americans is, that they think that they can exercise control. But the problem is, they don't know the cultures they are meddling with. Not everybody in the world follows their way of thinking. And that is why they run into continued problems. They want to force their will and worldview on other people. When that doesn't work, they are labelled 'undemocratic' and what not."

"How can they think that we are undemocratic? I have pointed out to them one hundred times what we believe in ..."

"They think they know better. They believe that you are a parochial warlord like many others, that you only want to hold on to your little fiefdom but otherwise do not have much of a plan nor ability to unite the country and stabilise it for their economic interests."

He shook his head.

"You are right, I am seeing it that way, too."

"We need to get out of them whatever possible and then have our own plan. We can't wait for them. We will see what the Europeans come up with ..."

During this time, we often only slept for three or four hours at night. Sometimes – especially when the military activities increased - I did not see Massoud for several weeks at a time as he was with his men at the front lines. Then of course his family demanded his attention, too.

In such cases, when we got back together, we did not talk about what happened at first. If we could be alone on the day we met again, we would often just cuddle up for a short while and hold each other, just be tender, often ended up making love. It was just us; the whole world would be outside of our door then.

In September 2000 we lost Taloqan to the Taliban, after a month of intense battle and over eight hundred of our fighters dead. It was a result of the disunity of the Front and our inability to raise enough funds above and beyond the limited American support to purchase weapons, ammunition, and other equipment. That whole year we had been in extremely bad shape financially.

By October, the Taliban had pushed our forces into the north-east of Afghanistan with the frontline now running from the Shomali Plain to the Khawaja Bahaudin district.

To break the situation Massoud planned a major offensive against their forces at Dasht-e-Qala.

Like the whole of northern Afghanistan, this area has several ancient historic sites, including one of the Alexandrias left behind by Alexander the Great's exploits in what was called Bakhtria in his days. At the confluence of the Kokcha and Panj River, both contributories to the Amu-Darya, is an excavation sites from the 1960 paying testimony to this ancient land. It is known by Ai-Khanum (Uzbek for "lady of the moon"). With the Soviet invasion, however, work there had to be abandoned and the site was subsequently looted. So, today, there is nothing much left to see there.

Together with the newly found alliance with the various pockets of resistance as described above, Massoud hoped to turn the situation in the resistance's favour even with the bad financial position we found ourselves in.

Still the situation had become very desperate, and we all were under great strain. More and more Massoud withdrew into his own thoughts; he surrounded himself only with his closest circle with whom he could discuss the situation as it developed. At the same time, he spent more and more time alone. I saw him often sitting alone, writing in his diary.

I would always be welcome, though, and no matter what distress tormented him, he would always welcome me with a heartfelt smile, affection pouring from his eyes. During this time, we grew even closer as he realised even more that I was there for him, no matter what.

One night in late October 2000 I could not sleep. It was two o'clock in the morning and I had tossed and turned for two hours. So, I decided to get up, and take a walk. I grabbed one of my kerosene lamps, threw on my pattoo and set off into the quiet, moon-light night. When I passed by Massoud's house I saw the light still on, so I knocked on his door, peeking through the gap asking "ejes'ast"[18] (may I come in)?

He sat at the table in the back. The woodstove was burning. With a kerosene lamp placed at the corner of the table he rested his head in his right hand and starred towards the drapes covering the window. When I knocked, he turned his head and looked at me in surprise.

"Of course!"

"I couldn't sleep" I explained without being asked.

I walked around the table to stand next to him, put my left arm around his shoulders and kissed his right cheek.

As I did so I noticed his cheek being moist and so I knew that just a short while ago tears had been running down his face. I felt a needle through my heart.

I caressed his cheek, then his hair and said:

"Please let me know what I can do to ease your pain."

He then dropped his head to the back and looked at me with his deep eyes.

---

[18] Literally: "is there permission?"

"Nothing, my darling, nothing. You are already doing more than I should ask you to."

I bent my head down to kiss him.

"The human character is terrible." He lamented "In times of need no one, except those who truly care for you, will stand by you."

"Come – do not strain yourself like that. Remember, I am going through the same struggle, I suffer with you, you know, I suffer with our people. But I still have hope that we will make it through somehow."

He got up and took my hands.

"Yah, InshAllah.".

"Did you lock the door?" he asked after a short silence.

"No – would you like me to?" I teased him, walking backwards towards the door giving him a cheeky smile.

"Yes ...." He smiled at me.

"I see." I turned the key.

He kept standing at the desk, watching me as I returned from the door. He wore a pair of beige trousers, a beige sweater over a dress shirt and simply looked handsome as always. His beautiful hair needed a cut, but I loved it when it was slightly longer, and the waves became more stubborn.

I walked up to him, stood very close. Then he put his arms around me, I put mine around his waist, raised my head and kissed him.

Also in late October 2000 J.B. together with the internationally acclaimed author Andrew Green and yet another National Geographic film crew returned to Afghanistan to join Massoud and his men at the front lines to document the crucial endeavour of a major counter-Taliban offensive across Northern Afghanistan, as described above, and produce a portrait of him. The documentary aired in early 2001.

Andrew Green was visibly shaken at the events he was witnessing. He had never seen the suffering which went on in the refugee-camps, he was never exposed to life fire at an actual front line. – At the same time, he was quite reserved vis-a-vie Massoud, trying to find an angle which allowed him to dampen the admiration the people who knew him showed. He appeared to make it his duty to find "the other side of the coin".

Of course, I spent a lot of time with them. Massoud, occupied with the offensive, had made me in charge of the crew when not at the front and asked me to bring them around and see to their every need. As was his habit he said that nothing was off-limits, they could film whatever they wanted.

They flew directly to Khawja Bahoudin and were scheduled to move on to Panjshir with Massoud a couple of days later.

"You have changed a lot, my dear" J.B. started the conversation while we were sitting in the little stone-walled house which was assigned to both Green and J.B.. "While you never struck me as a European even before, now you have become Afghan. Your Dari has become quite good, too." He smiled.

"Thank you, J.B." I replied in Dari

"Btw, do you know that you have taken up a bit of Amir Sahib's accent?" He smiled "It just struck me. Amazing!"

"Really? Wow, well, I mostly listen to him speak, so maybe no surprise there." I tried to make a funny face.

Massoud did not only grow up in the Panjshir, he also spent a couple of his teenage years in Herat as his father was stationed there as an army officer. Later the family moved back to Kabul where he attended the Lycée Isteqlal and later wanted to pursue training in a military academy to become an officer like his father. But with his parents against this career, he eventually started classes in engineering. So, due to the different locations, his accent was somewhat muddled.

"How do you manage to live here?" Green asked me "isn't it very hard, and even more so for a lady?"

"I have not really had a problem, you know. I loved it here from the beginning. Of course, there were a few things to get used to, and it is a harsh life, but I do not feel I am lacking anything. Also, and most importantly, when you are working with an incredible person like Massoud, you are equipped with incredible strength."

"Yes" Green said "I am sure"

"Let's not focus on me, anyway" I continued. "If you want to show Afghanistan's plight to the world, as you say, can I suggest that you visit the refugee camp in Panjshir and the one nearby here. You can talk to the IDPs [internally displace people] there – each story is worthwhile committing an hour to trust me. The camp in Panjshir – a little village it has become - is just at the entrance of the valley."

162

And so, when they accompanied Massoud a couple of days later down to Panjshir, J.B. in particular was shaken by the dreadful conditions in the camp, especially the children's situation concerned him deeply. Sick children everywhere – little could be done about it as there were far too few doctors in the area, if at all.

For days Massoud and his commanders stayed in bunkers during the operation and the film crew followed them. I never accompanied Massoud during such times – that would have been out of the question for many reasons, security and otherwise. Also, I would have been only a burden as I have no experience in such situations, not to mention have ever as so much fired a shot. So, my front-line experience of October 1997 remained my first and last one.

As always Massoud was heavily involved in the planning of the offensive and took a most dangerous flight over enemy lines with his helicopter to assess the situation. If they had been spotted, they could have easily been taken down by enemy fire. When I learned about his helicopter excursion, I said nothing, knowing that he would do it again, if necessary. His insurmountable courage which characterised him could not be broken, neither could his faith – both enabled him to do what he had been doing for the last twenty years.

So, when he returned from the offensive, which managed to push the Taliban back by some hard-earned kilometres, he was exhausted. For once he slept for ten hours, and when he got up the next day I had arranged for a large breakfast. When I got to his house at noon he was just finishing, sitting cross-legged on the floor with Abdullah.

163

Since we had not seen each other for two weeks I put on a simple beige kurta, slightly figure hugging, a pair of jeans and a coat, but I combined it with a beautifully imprinted chador which I wore in such a way that it showed more hair than usual. Of course, the usual make-up went on as well. I felt good. I felt pretty, pretty for my man.

When I walked through the door, I noticed with excitement that Massoud paused for a split second in the middle of his sentence when he raised his head and saw me entering. It was in the way he looked at me that showed that he was happy to see me and liked what he saw. Finding his train of thought back he turned to Abdullah again and finished his sentence.

"Salaam, sub bakhair" [good morning]

"Salaam, Ariana" replied Abdullah.

Despite the chilly temperature they had opened the door which led out onto the open field. It was a beautiful day, a typical Afghan sky. The sun was pouring in through the windows which were facing south. Overnight snow had fallen on the mountains in the distance, while the lower lying Khwaja Bahaudin area and the river where still snow free.

Massoud turned to me again.

"Ari[19], what did you have in mind with all that food? We did have things to eat out there, you know ..." he joked with a straight face, resting his elbows on his thighs, his

---

[19] After we got together, he started calling me either Ariana or Ari in private, or as is custom in Dari simply "Jaan" (dear). In the presence of people, other than his close friends, he always addressed me as "Khanum Ariana" (Madam) and with "shuma" (the formal version of "you"). I called him "Amir Sahib" at all time, and only when we were alone, "Ahmad", or also simply "Jaan". Massoud's close friends all called me "Ariana", everybody else "Khanum Ariana" or simply "Khanum".

characteristic shrug running down his right shoulder. He wore a coarse grey woollen sweater over his black kurta and salwar pants, Abdullah, as mostly, in grey western pants, woollen sweater and Kashmir jacket.

"I know, but not this. You looked in a terrible shape yesterday, so I thought you could do with a bit more energy than normal." I smiled at him

Amused, Abdullah pointed at the spot opposite him. "Sit, please. And thank you for all of this."

"See, at least Abdullah is thankful for what I did" I said, faking a serious mood.

"He is thankful for the both of us, so there is no need for me to be thankful" he replied in a dry fashion looking at Abdullah, while reaching for the tea kettle.

"I see", I tried hard to keep a straight face while snatching the pot away from him, poring tea for myself. "Abdullah, more tea?" I asked, ignoring Massoud.

"What's that cup for" I turned to him as he raised his cup signalling that I should fill it, too. Without complying I put down the kettle.

"Oh, I see, so you think you have done enough for me now?"

He gave me a cheeky yet so loving look which I reciprocated with a similar face.

Abdullah laughed, still he looked tired.

"How are things?" I finally started a serious conversation trying to look as relaxed as possible. Actually, I had been extremely worried and weary, going through restless nights with deep sleep evading me. The thought of losing him was unbearable.

"Overall, the operation was successful in the sense that the Taliban failed to make progress, in fact they had to retreat somewhat. The bad news was, though, that part of my orders on how and where to attack was not followed which resulted in several of our men being killed by landmines. It was so unnecessary and some of our young fighters lost their lives." Massoud said with lines crossing his forehead.

Both the men did not seem in the mood for long conversations, the past events kept them in a quiet mood, nursing their private thoughts.

After half an hour Abdullah got up and excused himself, leaving me and Massoud to finally talk in private.

"Ariana, I'll be with Arif in the foreign ministry" he said walking towards the door. "Come and see me later; then we can continue with our work on the Europe trip."

"Sure."

"You look very pretty, my darling" he began, smiling at me.

Was it not amazing? No man I had ever been with had such incredible burdens to carry, yet none of them was as observant as him, as much caring for and perceptive about a woman as him.

"Thanks. - I missed you." I smiled back at him. In place of a reply, he took my hand and kissed it.

"Ariana, what is going to become of us?" he asked me after a pause. "How are we going to beat this menace? I am so tired; I have been feeling this emptiness for months and I can't get rid of it …"

My heart quenched. I looked at him. Oh God – what was going through his mind, what desperation he must have felt?

I searched my brain for the right words, but I could not find any.

"I am not surprised. These are desperate times, and I am suffering with you — you know that. I have felt such emptiness before, too.

Only God can fill it. Pray from your heart, pray for guidance and God will tell you through your intuition."

"You are so right. God is the answer to everything. But maybe my faith is not strong enough sometimes."

"Even that He understands. He knows our struggles and temptations."

He looked at me with his handsome face.

"I was thinking of you a lot out there. I was thinking of how you swept into my life. How much you have become a part of me.

Tell me what I should be doing, my darling. All burdens are resting on my shoulders. Everybody relies on me. From guidance in the big frame down to details, even personal problems. I don't mind that, but it starts crushing me.

We have less and less time for each other, I have less and less time for my family. But it's not even that; things start slipping out of my hands. The enemies are too strong. I don't know anymore where to get the assistance from. And that is the truth. I never aimed at beating them militarily — that was never a feasible option — but I aimed at outlasting them, counting on aid from those people whose values we share — or so I thought. So far, we have been disappointed. You know the standpoint of the Americans. I have lost all hope that anything substantial is going to come from them. Their government situation is paralysed now. No one is going to take a decision in our favour, soon. I am worried that we get ground up between those wheels we have no control over."

What he said then has gone through my mind many times after his assassination as that was exactly what happened. He was left dangling between the egoistic interests of the various powers who had taken a stake in the future of Afghanistan.

"All I want is peace. I want to put my energy into building up this battered country not into fighting anymore.

I am tired, my darling, I am so tired."

He looked at me with his deep eyes, looking for an answer that could sooth his heart.

For the first time he showed me openly his exhaustion. It cut me deeply, tore at my heartstrings.

"Please give me all the work you can possibly load onto me" I replied "whatever you think I can do, I will do. Please tell me in detail what is on your mind, what are the detailed challenges.

Also, remember we are working on our Europe trip. If all goes well, I believe this can really make a difference."

"Yes, I know. And I really appreciate your work on that. I can't possibly give you more workload than you already have. I would feel very bad. You are already tearing yourself apart!"

He paused for a few seconds, staring out of the window.

Then he turned around and laid down on his back, resting his head in my lap. I caressed his hair with my right hand and put my other onto his stomach.

"I am leaving for Panjshir later", he said after a few long minutes of silence. "J.B. and the film crew are coming with me – I am planning to come back on Saturday."

"Yes, I remember."

He sat up. "Can you please keep on working with Abdullah on the Europe plans as we discussed?".

We got up, he picked up his patoo and wrapped it around his body and I put on my coat.

"Yes, of course" I took his left hand as we walked towards the door. "Be careful, please" I looked him in the eyes, then I wanted to quickly turn and leave, but he held my hand tightly and replied:

"I will – and if it's only for you."

I gave him a quick kiss, then turned and dropped the door close as I left. I did not want to spare any further thoughts on the fact that he was going to spend the next four days with his family, with his wife.

As I walked towards the "foreign ministry"[20], a building on a little hill, which we jokingly called this way because all of us working there were involved with international contacts and media matters, total joy swamped me.

It was late afternoon; the temperature was not above 10C and the mountains in the distance where tinged in a golden hue by the afternoon sun. As I stopped to look out over the wide-open landscape, wrapped in my coat and in the afterglow of the last hours, I felt warm and cosy in body and soul.

During the following four days Abdullah and I filled out the blanks as to what needed to be done over the next few months to prepare for our Europe trip. All we had in mind needed to be cross-referenced with our organisers in Europe

---

[20] the assassination of Massoud took place in this very building, with blood still splattered across the ceiling until today.

such as Ahmad Wali. So, we spent a fair bit of time on the phone.

J.B. and the crew had followed Massoud to the Panjshir, so I had no responsibilities with them during the next few days.

And in no time it was Saturday. By Friday evening it had gotten so cold, that I wore the thick Chinese army coat which I had bought years ago in Beijing where the winter temperatures are very similar to the foothills of the Hindu Kush. At night it was well below freezing and when stepping out of the house I wore long-johns below my salwar which was already made from warm winter material. If I did not wear my army coat, I wore another winter jacket with an Afghan style large shawl [pattoo] thrown over my shoulders. These keep very warm and cover most of the body.

In Khwaja Bahaudin most of the houses, including mine had a wood stove in the living area. But at night the fire would burn down, and it got very cold. So, one's day-clothes became more or less one's sleeping clothes as well. I would just take off the two outer layers and sleep in my long johns and shirt I was wearing below everything else. The bedding was very good, though. The duvet was very thick, so was the woollen blanket which covered it.

It was at around 11.00 pm that Saturday when I heard the door opening. I sat up in an instant, for a split-second thinking 'I should keep a gun next to my bed!'.

Trying to penetrate the dark with my eyes I heard the twitch of a match, then saw my kerosene lamp light up and Massoud putting down his pakul onto my table.

"Did I scare you?" he said in a soft voice

"Yes, a little" I gave him a relieved smile.

He sat down next to me and kissed me.

"I brought you a bag of dried mulberries". He pointed at the plastic bag on the table. He knew I loved them. Then he looked at me with a fatherly expression on his face.

"Are you alright? It has turned very cold, hasn't it?"

171

"I am fine."

He took my hand.

"It is so nice to know that you are here. That I can step into this house and find you here." He looked at me; after a pause he said:

"I brought you something else."

Another pause.

"You know that I can never marry you, right? – We have spoken of this. And yet, I want you to have this as a symbol of my love for you. I have been wanting to give this to you for a while, but first it took some time to make and then I was waiting for the right moment."

He pulled out a piece of white tissue paper from his pocket. When he unfolded the paper, it revealed a gold ring holding a small round piece of lapis lazuli like two prongs.

Letting the paper drop away he took my left hand and slipped the ring onto my ring finger. It fit perfectly.

"This little piece of lapis is my heart, and the two gold prongs are your hands." He raised his head and looked at me.

I was stunned.

"Oh God. You make me so happy ... oh God." I put my hands to his cheeks and kissed him. I was so taken aback.

"It is very beautiful. But you could have gotten me a can ring and I would have been just as happy" I let go of him and looked at the ring on my finger, extending my arm in front of me.

"Don't say anything – just wear it for the rest of your life." He looked at me with his serious face and deep eyes, caressing my left cheek.

Then he slipped off his boots, brought the lamp over and extinguished it. He lifted my blanket and moved in my direction, I making space for him.

"I just want to hold you. I need to feel you!" He turned to me and put his arms around me.

"You give me peace in this crazy life of mine. You make me forget all of this. When I am with you, it's just us. Your warm body, your sweet face, your beautiful mind and soul."

I turned around to kiss him. Softly, with all the love I felt for him.

With his arm around my waist, we fell asleep until 5 o'clock in the morning. Then he got up and left my house, leaving me to sleep for another hour.

This ring, which he had made in Pakistan from 20 karat gold with a stone from Badakhshan is the only thing I have left of him now, aside from the Christmas notes he left me each year. Everything else – his pakul, his watch, his diary, his books, everything that he owned is with his wife.

On 7th November J.B., Green and the film crew got ready to leave again.

During the last two days Abdullah, Massoud, J.B. and I took the opportunity to further discuss our Europe trip. J.B., of course being one of the organisers had lots of valuable input. At that stage he was still hopeful to arrange meetings with a whole range of high-calibre politicians. As the months went on, however, we had to take them off our list one by one until only a handful were left and ready to meet with our delegation.

Dust in the Wind
Europe 2001

3rd April 2001

It was a rainy, grey morning in the Panjshir Valley, with low-hanging clouds obscuring the mountains, when we boarded the Mi17 at 6.00 am bound for Dushanbe, Tajikistan. There we were scheduled to get on the private Aga Khan plane, which would fly us to Paris. The current Aga Khan, Shah Karim al-Husseini, had generously supported this trip.

Massoud's first visit to Europe had been a long time coming. Almost a year of preparations finally resulted in an invitation of the European Parliament for us to visit. Meetings with various representatives and dignitaries of the European Union in Paris, Brussels and Strasbourg were lined up for one week.

This visit came at a crucial and vulnerable time for us. The Taliban had made great advances around our territory and the main western power, the USA, had been continuing their support for Pakistan, enabling the latter to give massive logistical and man-power support to the Taliban. At the same time – as illustrated above – the CIA was ineffective in their efforts to gain more support for us in the new administration.

Massoud was very hopeful to start a turn in tide with this visit, a turn in tide which would make the international community withdraw direct or covert support for the Taliban and their backers.

I, however, was not too optimistic that we would achieve what we set out to do. The fact that several high-ranking officials were "out of town" during our visit, did not make it sound hopeful that Europe would adopt a pro-Northern Alliance policy which would affect our struggle positively, fast.

Never-the-less I felt it was worthwhile a shot. On hindsight, perhaps again maybe not as this visit may have stirred resentments in our camp which may have contributed to or at least did not prevent Massoud's assassination.

When we finally settled into our seats, I was already tired. Massoud and I, as well as several of our fellow travellers had not slept the whole night, still engaging in last-minute preparations. One of which was equipping Massoud with a passport.

We had his photo taken in Dushanbe, Fahim Dashty issuing the document as he was the keeper of the holy grail of official stamps of the Islamic Republic of Afghanistan.

Our party was composed out of only five delegates on the flight from Afghanistan: Massoud's close circle of the likes of Khalili and Abdullah. A host of other people, including some members of his family, would join us in Europe.

After take-off I settled into the big beige leather seats and slipped away easily into a deep sleep for two hours until they served us lunch.

When boarding the plane, I had picked a seat one row behind the men – this was official, so I wanted to stay on the sidelines as much as possible and left it to Massoud to engage with me at his choice – as we practiced it whenever in public.

When I woke up the sun was shining into my face and a sea of fluffy cotton clouds was displayed outside of my window. For the first time in days, I was excited about this trip – I had not been to Europe for ten years. Before I was going to return to Afghanistan, I planned to travel to Germany to visit my parents. For the last decade it had been them to visit me in Asia. Of course, they had received the shock of their life when I phoned them before my departure from Singapore in September 1997 about my plans of joining a television crew to Afghanistan. Nothing, however, had prepared them for the news that I had decided to stay on in this war-torn country to fight "other people's war" as my father put it. Now after three years of regular phone calls they were still in utmost alarm but were starting to deal with it.

After I finished my meal Abdullah joined me with a smile: "How are you doing – everything alright?" He spoke in English.

"Yap, everything o.k.

Is Amir Sahib not eating?" I asked him seeing Massoud's tray still untouched.

"He is still sleeping. - How are you both getting on?" he asked after a pause.

"Heaven, Abdullah, heaven." I replied smiling at him. "I have never worked so much and slept so little in my whole life, but I have also never been so deeply happy. "

"I am glad to hear it. I always wish you the best."

"Thank you."

When Massoud awoke he asked the flight attendant for some water then slowly began eating his meal. When he was finished, he turned to Khalili who sat next to him in the aisle-seat and asked where I was. Khalili turned around and pointed in my direction signalling me to come over.

"Ariana, sit here – keep my company" Massoud smiled at me pointing at the empty window seat opposite him. He looked tired; he would look tired for this whole visit. All his energy and hope had gone into it, and it exhausted him. He looked aged by ten years at times sometimes.

Khalili got up and made his way to the toilet – Afghans have this great sense of privacy. Khalili, too, must have known by now about our relationship. Respecting his friend, he accepted it just like Abdullah.

Leaving all public initiatives to Massoud put me out of the spot and left it to him to blur the lines.

"Have you made any more changes to our agenda with the European Parliament President?"

"No, I just felt that we should cover a few more points such as ..."

And so we spent the next couple of hours leafing through papers, wording and re-wording documents.

We landed in Paris at 4.00 pm local time, half an hour later we sat in our cars after being hurried through the diplomatic channel. I shared a black BMW with Abdullah, our local Omaid Weekly editor and the Press Attaché of the European Parliament who had met us at the airport.

Massoud, Khallili, and Afghanistan's representative to the United Nations in Geneva, Humayun Tandar, boarded the other BMW. The rest of our delegation was to meet us in the hotel.

We were whisked off into downtown Paris where we checked into the Hotel Le Crillion, one of the finest addresses in town, near the Place de la Concorde. Each of us had a room to ourselves, Massoud had been given a suite with a separate bed- and living room – Wali and the other organisers in Europe went overboard in my opinion, but of course the hotel was absolutely stunning. Modern design mixed with elegant opulent architectural details made it indeed one of the first addresses in Paris.

Several European journalists including J.B., Rafaele Ciriello and Christophe de Ponfilly as well as a few of their colleagues, who had been essentially the ones to push this trip for us, had organised a small dinner in Massoud's suite that evening. Wali and our entourage thus gathered there with them at about 8 pm.

This was the first time I met Ahmad Wali in person. Amazing how two brothers can be so different in both appearance and demeanour! Wali being a nice-enough person, had none of his brother's eloquence, charm, and charisma. Yet he is open and friendly and likes to talk – a lot. I had had frequent contact with him on the phone and was impressed with his English. No surprise, since he had been living in London for over ten years.

J.B. was very happy to meet me again and for a while we just retreated into one corner of the suite to chat, and I had the chance to give him a good run-down on how things were going in Afghanistan.

"I am planning on coming to Afghanistan again in August. I want to start an NGO there that teaches journalists and photographers. I also want to do something to educate the children. This has no clear shape yet, but something along those lines ..."

"That's great ... let me know when the time comes, maybe I can help ... despite Taliban and all."

How terribly surprising life can be! He did not know at this point that he would be seeing Massoud for the last time that week in France because when he came to Kabul in August, he did not find time to meet with him, and in September the Lion of Panjshir would already be dead! Little did I know that this NGO would become my home thereafter.

After we had all gathered, Massoud got up and addressed us all in a very moving speech, translated by J.B.

"I want to take this opportunity to deeply thank you all for making this trip possible." He said in a quiet voice, uncertain about his words, looking straight at us, letting his eyes circle the round. "I deeply value your friendship and engagement with our cause. It has been very inspirational for me to see foreigners like you – and only one of you has merged to become Afghan" – he looked at me with a smile, as I was standing with J.B. near the open fireplace – "to put in all this effort for us. We all much appreciate that and will never forget it. May this be a watershed for Afghanistan!"

This whole week was filled with travelling – by private plane and road trips - to Strasburg and Brussels, with lunches, dinners, and meeting after meeting with our delegation stressing, re-iterating and patiently dissecting again and again our points about the situation in Afghanistan, the involvement of foreign powers, the Taliban, our vision for the Afghan society and many more. Urging the western countries to undermine the drive and support of the Taliban and their Pakistani backers, Massoud did not ask for military support but for a political breakdown of those forces. He also asked for humanitarian aid to be channelled to the refugees.

In Paris, Strasburg, and Brussels, he met with understanding everywhere – or so it seemed. His winning, intelligent personality and warm charisma opened doors with everybody. His speeches and conversations were full of drive and fervour for his cause.

This was our schedule:

04 April 2001

Our first meetings were held in Paris with French Foreign Minister Hubert Vedrine followed by the National Assembly President Raymond Forni and finally with Senate Speaker Christian Poncelet.

05 April 2001

We flew to Strasburg for a meeting with Nicole Fontaine, the president of the European Parliament and a question-and-answer session in front of the International Affairs Committee of the European parliament.

In the afternoon we held a press conference.

06 – 07 April 2001

We drove to Brussels for consultations with the European Commission, represented by Javier Solana (high representative for security and foreign policy at time).

Here we were originally supposed to meet with Commission President Romano Prodi, External Affairs Commissioner Chris Patten or Development and Humanitarian Aid Commissioner Paul Nielson, but they were all out of town on Friday, as we were told ahead of time.

As J.B. would write in his 2002 photo book 'Massoud': "Dans ses yeux j'ai vu de la deception", I too, saw the disappointment in his eyes, even though he said:

"I guess there is nothing we can do – as long as we can make an impact."

Instead, the main event was a meeting with Belgian Foreign Minister Louis Michel on the 7th.

Without having planned it that way on purpose, I turned out to be the one having to be in five places at the same time. Massoud wanted me to be with him everywhere, he called me in on many things. At the same time many people, especially the press, was interested in my persona.

I spoke to all liaison personnel, I ended up as interpreter a couple of times, having to toggle between German, English, French, and Dari.

I was flying on high. While sometimes my head was spinning, I enjoyed the buzz, I enjoyed paving the way for him, I enjoyed being seen as his right hand.

During lunches I would still be on the phone or entertain people who addressed me on this or the other matter. I would always sit at his table together with other members of our party. The only woman, but no one seemed to bother. No one from the Afghan side as I had become so much part of the scene over the last three years and no one from the European side anyway as no one would give such matters a second thought.

Having spoken to most people before-hand out of Afghanistan people remembered my name so I was the referral point, next to Abdullah of course, everybody fell back on.

I had not only been given a local mobile phone but also a walkie-talkie, which enabled me to stay in touch with the security personnel of for example the European Parliament president in Strasburg. Once the respective person had arrived, I silenced those devices in order to be able to concentrate on the meeting itself.

During one of the lunches, in Brussels, I had a few minutes without interruption so I could dedicate myself to some food. I got up and scanned the buffet. When I returned with my plate, I noticed Massoud looking at me. I looked back at him with a smile and instead of sitting at my original spot I moved to the empty chair next to him.

"Did you switch off your phones?" he asked me.

"I can't do that. Sorry."

"I hope we can meet later some place alone – I need to rest my brain.

You must be tired, too. You work so hard," he said in French "So many people and so many appointments. But it's of course good for us."

"As you know we have one meeting with the Belgium Foreign Minister this afternoon 'for tea', as that was so nicely put. So that means that it will be in an intimate circle, five people tops. It should not be more than two hours. After that we could take five – either we meet in your suite or step out for a walk what do you think?"

"Yes, let's do that." He smiled at me.

At that moment Humayun Tandar stepped up to Massoud and started a conversation. Smiling at me, he apologised for interrupting.

At the same moment my phone rang. It was one of the European Parliaments Press Officers. I moved two chairs over.

I liked those small meetings, like the one with Louis Michel, the Belgian Foreign Minister.

I could still not believe the fact that I was part of all this, that Massoud brought me along all the time and involved me in answering some questions. If he did not involve me, I stayed quiet, instead seeing to little comforts of our group such as filling the cups, telling people to alter the room temperature etc.

It was Massoud, Abdullah, Michel, his translator, his secretary and I. The discussion was very frank and candid, with Michel showing intense interest in the strategy of the United Front after a potential victory. I deduced from that that he represented a camp which doubted the ability of any successors to the Taliban to be able to hold on to power – a repeat of the situation of 1992 to 1996. But Massoud won the argument. Of course, he did. How could anyone not see that he had a well-developed vision for Afghanistan and that he had learned from the mistakes committed in the mid-nineties?

In response to Massoud's elaborations Michel said: "The international community and Belgium will do their best to help the Northern Alliance in his fight for his people, to reach a cease-fire between all rival parties and to organize free elections for men and women."

He further mentioned plans for an educational program for Afghan women, who had been systematically stripped of their rights since the Taliban came into power in 1996, closing all schools to women, denying them access to hospitals and barring them from working outside the home.

Michel also condemned the Taliban for their seeming indifference to Afghan opium cultivation and for harbouring terrorists like Bin Laden. He added "suspected" here. I didn't like this politically correct phrasing. To me it was one of the subtle signs of distancing oneself from the issue at hand.

Pakistan's role in the Afghan civil war was also addressed and the Foreign Minister signalled his understanding of Massoud's position in this matter.

Michel pledged to reinforce humanitarian aid on a European level for Afghan refugees in Pakistan and Iran. Going forward, non-governmental organizations would be sent directly into Afghanistan without passing through Pakistan. At the same time he signalled his country's preparedness to put more pressure on Pakistan politically.

After the meeting with Louis Michel, we managed to take a break as planned. We had two hours until at seven o'clock we would meet the president of the European Parliament, Nicole Fontaine, and a few of her colleagues for dinner.

Since it looked like rain, we ended up going to his suite. I went to my room first, alone, waiting for our delegation to leave Massoud. After I received his "all clear" phone call I joined him.

"Would you like something to eat or drink?" I asked him

"No, I'm good." He smiled, walked up to me, held my head in his hands and kissed me.

"It seems like ages I have touched you. For one week we have not been alone – do you realise that?"

I put my arms around his waist.

I had observed him often during the last few days and I was so proud of being with him, having the relationship I had with him. I felt this tremendous attraction, he was such a man! His hair turning grey, his sharp features, his beautiful eyes, his intelligent face, his demeanour, the way he spoke to and interacted with people, his entire personality. Oh God, how my love for him had grown deeper in the last couple of years. So deep that when he left me, it tore my heart apart, cracking my whole being with irreparable damage.

It was six o'clock when I stepped out of the suite and left Massoud to rest for another hour.

I first went to my room to have a shower and change for the dinner. I put on an Indian dress with ancle-length, figure-hugging short-sleeve kurta and churidar pants, pink colour, intricate flower design, beautiful chiffon chador, matching bangles, matching earrings, and choker. It was one of those days when you love yourself, when your hair is just nice, when your skin has not one blemish and your clothes feel sown to your body. I felt beautiful – not for anybody else but for my man.

I then went down to the dining room where the dinner was held, with my chador thrown front to back over my shoulders, covering the front of my upper body.

There were still some details to be ironed out before the dinner, so some other members of our delegation joined me to settle them. Most of them had never seen me dressed that way, with uncovered hair and short sleeves – so I could see the look on their faces, trying not to stare.

Abdullah arrived ten minutes before the rest of our delegation. He looked very smart in his dark-blue dinner suit.

"Are they going to remove those flowers? You know that Khalili will die of an allergy attack if they leave them on the table?" he made a funny face

"Yes, I know" I laughed back at him "I already told the catering supervisor."

When Massoud finally arrived then with the rest of our delegation, I met him in the foyer. When he first noticed me, something in his eyes told me that he liked what he saw.

"Nicole Fontaine just arrived."

As he walked next to me towards the dinner venue he bent over and whispered in French:

"You look amazing, my darling."

Nicole Fontaine was one of the genuinely interested politicians we met on this trip. She was personally impressed with Massoud, he had captured her, one could see that. If she had not been some ten years older than him, I would have been jealous at the way she spoke to him: full of attention, absorbing every word, not missing one opportunity to smile at him.

She ended up being one of the few who in the wake of the visit tried to push for serious action on the Afghanistan situation but was unable to make a difference. After his assassination she voiced deep grief and shock at the loss of "this brave man." She got involved with the Massoud Foundation, which, however, so far did not gain the profile it could have gained.

With the action continuing for a straight week Massoud sometimes looked exhausted, his eyes far away. Whenever my direct involvement was not required I had time to observe him - so - despite his otherwise strong showing - when I saw him sitting in those big armchairs, or behind yet another white clothed table, looking somewhat misplaced in his khaki outfit and pakul, his communication hampered by the constant involvement of translators, I knew that this was one of the last momentous efforts he would make; somehow an indescribable sadness fell onto me – maybe it was a premonition of things to come or simply the notion of seeing him age before his time.

On 4th of April, still in Paris, after the aforementioned appointments, there was also a secret meeting taking place between Massoud and the CIA.

Gary Schroen and Richard Blee had flown in. During the meeting they tried to reassure Massoud that even though the pace of their visits to Panjshir had slowed because of the policy gridlock in Washington, the CIA still intended to keep up its regular instalment payments of several hundred thousand dollars as part of their intelligence-sharing arrangements. They also wanted to know how Massoud felt about his military position.

Massoud told them that he thought he could defend his lines in the northeast of Afghanistan, but that was about all. The United States had to do something, or eventually he was going to crumble.

Other than that, there had been no meetings lined up in the late afternoon of 4th April and so we all had some breathing time. So, I decided to retire to my room and take it easy.

The rooms of the Hotel de Crillon where just breath-taking – modern furniture combined with Second Empire architectural detail. The bed was an old four-poster king-size bed, with laced bed linen and loads of pillows.

I took a bath, then wrapped myself in the fluffy bathrobe, sat on the bed, ordered a nice cup of French coffee and a couple of croissants from room-service, and watched television. After a while I got bored of it and just dosed off on the bed.

About half an hour later I heard a knock on my door. Since our floor was guarded by security personnel, I readily opened the door. It was Massoud.

"How did you get away? Did you bribe your guard?"

"I walked out of the door …" came the cheeky reply so typical of him.

"Really? Amazing." I shot back at him with a straight face and sat down on the bed.

He laughed.

"I just told everybody that I would like to be alone for a while. So, I believe that they are all mostly downstairs in the coffee house. I told the guard at my door not to let visitors know that I left."

He sat next to me on the bed, and I turned to him with one leg folded on the bed the other on the floor.

He reached out and took my hands.

"Thank you for all your hard work. Everything seems to be going so well. You are so great with the people here; they all love and admire you for working with us. I received so many comments."

"How can I not work hard for you. You mean everything to me, and Afghanistan is my life now."

He moved away from me and stretched out on the bed.

"Do you want to eat something?" I asked him. "Let's order something from room-service, o.k.? They are very fast – I tried it earlier."

"O.k. – how about some croissants – I can't get enough of them. I think we should open a French bakery in Kabul after the Taliban are chased out, what do you think?"

"You are sweet – I can just picture you as the head-baker. But, yah, great idea. If that doesn't work, we revert to your original idea of a carpet laying business. Since you have already hands-on experience in fitting carpet-flooring …" I teased him. He laughed. "Absolutely!"

190

I was referring to the fact that he was just about to finish his new house in Panjshir and had done some of the decorating work himself such as laying the fitted carpet in the living room and his study. This was the first property which he actually owned himself. Prior to that he and his family had always lived in his in-laws' house just below, a much more modest building than what he had helped design now. When doing the carpeting work, he had to borrow a cutting knife from a relative and upon returning it joked that in case the government-job did not work out he actually had a future as a carpet cutter.

I rang room service, who must have thought that I am suffering from a croissant addiction, and 10 minutes later we had a tray with four croissants and a kettle of tea in front of us (I could never warm him to coffee – it made him nervous he said).

After pouring the tea for him, I broke off a piece of croissant and put it to his mouth.

After he finished one croissant, he moved the tray from the bed onto the coffee table and stretched out on the bed again. "Come" he reached for me. I laid down next to him and put my arm around his torso.

So here we were in this fluffy European bed in Paris, at five in the afternoon – expanded between the pages of time. - We did not belong here, yet we had to be here to secure our survival. Floating on a cloud above the realpolitik of this trip we were lost in our affection for each other. A relationship un-pressured by time, un-pressured by anything – we just always lived it day by day, squeezed into the gaps his life had left for us.

"What is your feeling about this trip? Do you feel it will make a difference?" he asked after he had sat up and poured the remaining tea.

"To be honest – I am not sure. The stones of change grind slowly. Even if there are countries now that will suspend support to Pakistan etc, I am not sure whether it will be fast enough. The net of dependencies is quite complex, and I worry that they will sacrifice us in their game … honestly this is what I think. So, let's work on a back-up plan"

"Maybe you are too pessimistic. I'm getting the impression that we are making some impact here."

"Yes, we are. But will it ring home? Enough to make a difference to us. You see, what I disliked from the start was that several high-calibre government representatives are not available to meet us. That means on a very official level the EU does not want to be seen to be too closely affiliated with us while at the same time they can't outright reject us because towards their people they can't be seen supporting the Taliban either. – Also, the fact that it was mentioned several times that they want to give humanitarian aid to all sides, seems a typical diplomatic move which does not commit them.

That means they will want to tread carefully, which again means too slow of an action for us."

He gave me one of his long thoughtful looks which I knew meant that I had broken his previous train of thought.

"We will have to see. But I urge you to come up with a concise back-up plan, which does not count on foreign support other than support we can be one hundred percent sure of. We need to give the Taliban a fatal blow soon otherwise I worry this will be our last season hunting."

"You are probably right" he finally replied, chewing on his last bite. "But let's not view this too negatively, either. The press conference tomorrow is important, too. I am particularly counting on your impact. But, yes, as in life, one should never count on other people's support. One can only trust oneself at the end of the day."

"Not quite true – you can rely on me one hundred percent – I hope you know that."

"Yes, of course I do – but you are an exception in many ways. In every way, actually." He smiled and caressed my right cheek.

"Let's get moving. Join me in a while in my room and call the others from downstairs, o.k.? I want to go through the press conference details again with you all."

With this he took my hand and held it while he walked away from me. I got up, walked with him a few steps, then stopped; when he reached the door, he let his hand slip out of mine.

That evening we all gathered as planned in Massoud's suite.

After he had left my room, I had gone to the hotel lobby to find our party. I found them all gathered in one of the sofa corners of the big coffee shop. When I approached, Abdullah saw me, but I signalled him to stay quiet as I wanted to play a joke on Khaliii who, sitting on one of the beige armchairs facing a huge plush purple sofa, had his back turned towards me and was gesturing wildly. The others followed my signal, too. Khalili was in the midst of complaining about this and the other person among the Northern Alliance parties and just finished his sentence with "all this pride will bring us down one day.", when I tapped him on the shoulder and said "That's right. And that is why more women must run

Afghanistan. Then there won't be all these testosterone driven arguments ..."

Shocked Khalili swivelled his head around, looked at me, speechless for a split second, then laughed.

"Yes, you are right. Particularly if there were lots of women like you. – Sit, please." He said after he recovered, got up and urged me to sit in his chair.

I refused, instead sitting down on an empty small ottoman next to him.

"We did not see you all afternoon. What did you do?"

"Sleep" I replied while sitting down, unable of course to tell them what I really did. "I was so tired. Politics is tiring, talking to people is tiring.

If you all are ready, perhaps we can go upstairs. Amir Sahib informed me that he wants us all in his suite to go through the anticipated topics to come up during meeting at the parliament tomorrow and the press conference after that."

Once everybody settled down, Abdullah listed a few popular topics and everybody joined in with ideas on how to answer them, on how to best present our views and on how to counter objections.

As far as the press conference, which was to follow in the afternoon, was concerned, Massoud wasted no time in making it clear that he thought it would be best if I were the central mediator given my background and because I was a woman.

I felt somewhat exposed – yes, the idea was a good one and made strategic sense, but at the same time it became so clear at that moment that he wanted the two of us to be a team, visible to everybody. And we were – I just was not sure at that stage whether it was a good moment to demonstrate it. It somehow occurred to me that the time we had spent that afternoon underlined the bond he felt for me, that I had proved to him even more than before that I was to be trusted one hundred percent.

It was about 9pm when we finished. Since it was not quite bedtime yet, I had not eaten anything since the croissants and because I had taken a nap in the afternoon, I did not feel tired. So, I asked J.B. whether we wanted to step out and get a drink and have something to eat. He agreed and so we went to a small wine place not far from the hotel.

"You are doing an amazing job" he began as we sat down.

"Thank you – do your really think so?"

"Well, I know that it was mainly you who organised the details from Afghanistan, who hooked up with the relevant people etc.

Massoud knows that, too. Just now I was amazed to see how the both of you are working together. I can see a very strong bond between you two. Already when we came to Khwaja Bahaudin last year, I could see that. I have never seen anyone in his circle over the last 16 years that I have known him who seemed so on par with him, so quietly agreeing on most things."

"Well, first of all I'm by far not the main actor here. Without you and your journalist colleagues this would not have been possible.

But yes, J.B., yes, my dream has come true; and I know it is wrong, but it has been overwhelming from the beginning and it still is, growing stronger by the day. Do you think it is very obvious?"

"Not to someone who does not know either one of you well. You behave very discretely, that's for sure."

"Did he ever tell you anything?"

"No – men would not do that – I think nowhere in the world; particularly not if it is such a sensitive subject. But I knew straight away when we came to Afghanistan last November. Your eyes, my dear, you could never conceal your eyes. But he, too, gives these signals. You see, I know him well, I have observed his behaviour patterns for sixteen years. When he interacts with you, he becomes very soft and kind, his face lights up. Not that he otherwise is rude or anything like that, but with you he interacts in a special manner. He will leave anyone standing and turn his attention to you." He laughed.

"The funny thing is" he continued "when I told him about your request to stay on, I told him about my concern of you being an attractive woman. And you know what he said?"

"Yes, I know what he said: 'I can handle it' – right?"

"Oh, so he told you about it. Yes, that's what he said. But I knew when he agreed to you staying on, it was partially because he had already fallen for you – perhaps not admitting to it yet."

"Yes, I believe so, too. -

You know, after knowing him and experiencing this relationship - extraordinary in every way - I have had my fill of life. I am ready to die tomorrow. I have experienced pure happiness. Anything better than that can only happen beyond this world."

"You are amazing – actually, you know, you both are. You both are very different – of extraordinary mental and emotional strength.

Now that we know each other a bit better I can tell you this: when you first approached me in Singapore and showed this incredible dedication for Massoud and his cause I first thought that you are one of those Europeans who do not quite know what they are talking about and that a certain level of romance had taken over your rational thinking. But now I am glad that I gave you the benefit of a doubt."

"So rude!" I faked distress "I should punish you for that; I feel it's appropriate now that you buy me another glass of wine" I smiled at him.

"Mademoiselle – encore un verre, s'il vous plait."

"Maybe we won't have time to say good-bye tomorrow – things tend to get very hectic. So, here's to our friendship and that we may meet again soon." I toasted to him

"I'll be in Kabul in August – hopefully I find time to visit you."

"Insh Allah"

"Insh Allah" he smiled.

The most crucial day was the 5th of April where we first had the opportunity to speak to the Foreign Affairs Committee and other interested parties of the European Parliament, presided over by Nicole Fontaine.

Massoud had not been invited to speak in the plenum, a fact which, in my eyes, also demonstrated the more hesitant stance official Europe had taken vis-à-vis our cause.

Massoud sat at the centre of the long multi-chair row facing the committee on an elevated platform, flanked by Abdullah and Mdm Fontaine. Abdullah acted as his while all other participants were translated through their headphones via the parliament's translation service.

I remained in the background at this occasion, following everything from an empty seat in the auditorium.

In the afternoon we held the said press conference with many Afghan and international media outlets present. It was the occasion to make public again what we had discussed and re-iterated with all the representatives we had met so far.

As decided, I gave a brief address to the media before Massoud spoke and took questions. It was hoped that this would give an additional publicity and credibility boost.

The press conference was a huge success.

It was held in Strasburg in an adjacent building of the European Parliament. More than five hundred journalists took part.

Already an hour before the start the room was packed to the brim with journalists. They had underestimated the turn up and not even all our delegation had a place to sit.

At three o'clock we closed the doors and I got up from my chair and tapped on the microphone. After several seconds the voices died down. I gave it another two seconds before I began. I had chosen to wear a Piran Tombon but instead of a head scarf I wore a pakul. It made me feel good, proud to represent this adopted cause of mine, which had so much become a part of me.

"You look cute in this" Massoud had commented just before we entered the press conference room.

"Cute? Cute is defined as 'ugly but adorable' – is that what you mean?"

"No, just adorable ..." he smiled at me.

As we settled down in our chairs behind a long table in front of the crowd of journalists, the Afghan black-white-and-green flag behind us, I took a minute just to let my eyes wander, taking in the fact that I was here, with him, arguing the cause of Afghanistan. I zoomed in on different people, trying to guess what they might be thinking. Many of them still adjusting their equipment, others already making notes. Would the foreigners among them ever really understand what all this meant? Who Massoud was? To most of them, this would just stay another conflict which sooner or later would be handled somehow.

"Bismillah, Rahman e Rahim! [in the name of God, the merciful, the compassionate]

Ladies and gentlemen, it is an honour for us to stand in front of you today and to be able to answer your questions about Afghanistan and the goals of the Northern Alliance. Ahmad Shah Massoud will be taking your questions after this. Please direct them to me in English, French or German and I will

199

translate for Amir Sahib. All those able to speak Urdu, Dari and Pashto may address him directly.

I am personally not worthy of speaking of the needs and struggle of Afghanistan and her people as I did not personally endure the hardship of the Afghans of the last 20 years. I only joined their cause four years ago. By contrast, all men present here today have greatly suffered and sacrificed a large part of their lives for the well-being of the Afghan people. Hence, rather than making my own words I would like to read out an address which Amir Sahib had sent to the Foreign Policy Committee of the United States of America in 1998. Unfortunately, not much has changed in the Western approach to Afghanistan ever since, which is why I can now read it out to you with the same validity as in 1998.

Thus, we urge the governments of Europe not to stand back from the necessary action once more.

Al Queda and the Taliban are not a problem restricted to Afghanistan or the Middle East. They are aiming for global dominance and as such may soon attack the West, too. How, we do not know, when, we don't know, but they have means at their disposal with the potential of great destruction.

So, helping Afghanistan means acting in self-preservation.

In the name of God

Mr. Chairman, honourable representatives of the people of the United States of America,

I send this message to you today on behalf of the freedom and peace-loving people of Afghanistan, the Mujahedeen freedom fighters who resisted and defeated Soviet communism, the men and women who are still resisting oppression and foreign hegemony and, in the name of more than one and a half million Afghan martyrs who sacrificed their lives to uphold some of the same values and ideals shared by most Americans and Afghans alike. This is a crucial and unique moment in the history of Afghanistan and the world, a time when Afghanistan has crossed yet another threshold and is entering a new stage of struggle and resistance for its survival as a free nation and independent state.

I have spent the past 20 years, most of my youth and adult life, alongside my compatriots, at the service of the Afghan nation, fighting an uphill battle to preserve our freedom, independence, right to self-determination and dignity. Afghans fought for God and country, sometimes alone, at other times with the support of the international community. Against all odds, we, meaning the free world and Afghans, halted and checkmated Soviet expansionism a decade ago. But the embattled people of my country did not savour the fruits of victory. Instead they were thrust in a whirlwind of foreign intrigue, deception, great-gamesmanship and internal strife. Our country and our noble people were brutalized, the victims of misplaced greed, hegemonic designs and ignorance. We Afghans erred too. Our shortcomings were as a result of political innocence, inexperience, vulnerability, victimization, bickering and inflated egos. But by no means does this justify what some of our so-called Cold War allies did to undermine this just victory and unleash their diabolical plans to destroy and subjugate Afghanistan.

Today, the world clearly sees and feels the results of such misguided and evil deeds. South-Central Asia is in turmoil, some countries on the brink of war. Illegal drug production, terrorist activities and planning are on the rise. Ethnic and religiously motivated mass murders and forced displacements are taking place, and the most basic human and women's rights are shamelessly violated. The country has gradually been occupied by fanatics, extremists, terrorists, mercenaries, drug Mafias and professional murderers. One faction, the Taliban, which by no means rightly represents Islam, Afghanistan or our centuries-old cultural heritage, has with direct foreign assistance exacerbated this explosive situation. They are unyielding and unwilling to talk or reach a compromise with any other Afghan side.

Unfortunately, this dark accomplishment could not have materialized without the direct support and involvement of influential governmental and non-governmental circles in Pakistan. Aside from receiving military logistics, fuel and arms from Pakistan, our intelligence reports indicate that more than 28,000 Pakistani citizens, including paramilitary personnel and military advisers are part of the Taliban occupation forces in various parts of Afghanistan. We currently hold more than 500 Pakistani citizens including military personnel in our POW camps. Three major concerns - namely terrorism, drugs and human rights - originate from Taliban-held areas but are instigated from Pakistan, thus forming the inter-connecting angles of an evil triangle. For many Afghans, regardless of ethnicity or religion, Afghanistan, for the second time in one decade, is once again an occupied country.

Let me correct a few fallacies that are propagated by Taliban backers and their lobbies around the world. This situation over the short and long-run, even in case of total control by the Taliban, will not be to anyone's interest. It will not result in stability, peace, and prosperity in the region. The people of Afghanistan will not accept such a repressive regime. Regional countries will never feel secure and safe. Resistance will not end in Afghanistan, but will take on a new national dimension, encompassing all Afghan ethnic and social strata.

The goal is clear. Afghans want to regain their right to self-determination through a democratic or traditional mechanism acceptable to our people. No one group, faction or individual has the right to dictate or impose its will by force or proxy on others. But first, the obstacles have to be overcome, the war has to end, just peace established and a transitional administration set up to move us toward a representative government.

We are willing to move toward this noble goal. We consider this as part of our duty to defend humanity against the scourge of intolerance, violence and fanaticism. But the international community and the democracies of the world should not waste any valuable time, and instead play their critical role to assist in any way possible the valiant people of Afghanistan overcome the obstacles that exist on the path to freedom, peace, stability and prosperity. Effective pressure should be exerted on those countries who stand against the aspirations of the people of Afghanistan. I urge you to engage in constructive and substantive discussions with our representatives and all Afghans who can and want to be part of a broad consensus for peace and freedom for Afghanistan.

With all due respect and my best wishes for the government and people of the United States,

Ahmad Shah Massoud."

Thank you.

And now Ahmad Shah Massoud would like to make an updated statement to the world, hoping that it may be taken seriously."

With this I switched off my microphone, and handed the word over to my man, so that he could make a prepared statement.

In it he put the blame of the Taliban's strength in Afghanistan squarely on the support from Pakistan and their American backers and lamented once more the lack of Western support for his alliance. Once more he urged the West to change their approach to Afghanistan and see the bigger problems associated with it.

It ended with these prophetic words which give me and others the goosebumps every time we think of it:

"My message to President Bush is that the war in Afghanistan and the presence of terrorist bases will not only remain limited to Afghanistan but that sooner or later these threats will also target the United States and many other countries in the region and throughout the world. If

you do not help us rid our land of those terrorists who have invaded it, there will be a disaster, a horror visited up on without comprehension and endurance. So, in helping us, help yourselves."

Of course, we had heard chatter on the wind that Al Quaida was planning to make a big statement, that something big might be going down. Our spies had a wide reach. But we did not know what, nor when or who. Because it was just that: chatter.

Massoud's warning was therefore more rooted in a general knowledge of the aspiration to world-domination harboured by Al Qaida, rather than concrete intelligence. Therefore, nothing was intentionally withheld from the West.

After that I was first bombarded with questions about my persona, as could have been expected. That was very welcome, as we hoped that would generate more interest in Afghanistan. I answered some of those myself – Massoud most of them. But he would always turn to me, seeking my approval for whatever he said about me. While I sat there nodding at what he told the press or translating for him I was bursting with pride.

As far as the Afghan representatives in the crowd, the press conference at times turned more into a town-hall event rather than a press conference, with some of the speakers having to be reminded to cut their elaborations short and ask a question.

Massoud's spirited answers drew a lot of applause from the audience.

When we left France on 8th April, we thought we had achieved the attention to Afghanistan which was required to rally the necessary support. However, and in short: we did not. None of the European countries followed through with action on the insights they allegedly gained. Humanitarian aid was approved and provided. But political consequences remained wanting.

When pressure on the USA finally gained momentum to drop the covert support for the Taliban it was already too late for the US herself – the evil plan of the World Trade Centre attacks had already been hatched and was close to execution. As for Afghanistan the only obstacle in the Taliban's and their backers' way was Ahmad Shah Massoud – unprotected in an enclave just covering no more than 10% of the country he and his allied forces had been battling an enemy enjoying support from far greater sources than Massoud's – yet they could not break him. So, they killed him.

Until today there is no conclusive proof as to who the killers were. It is widely assumed, but not proven, that they were Al-Qaida members acting at the direct orders of Bin Laden.

A conspiracy from a much less suspected angle may, however, be considered just the same: Ahmad Shah Massoud did not only stand in the way of the Taliban and Al-Qaida and their Muslim Kalifate but also in the way of Unicol and other oil companies and their Central Asian oil-pipeline projects as well as the US's ambitions to appease Afghanistan at any price to warrant for safe access to Central Asia. Political murder becomes a viable option if it can go un-prosecuted amidst the lawlessness.

It can be assumed, too, that Massoud as de facto leader of his alliance was not supported by the US and other Western powers because he had an agenda of independence for a post-war Afghanistan and was less than inclined to lean towards any power, but certainly not more than necessary towards the US. If he had become President of Afghanistan, he would have been a harder nut to crack than someone who was already familiar with the American way and had not fought any battles for the country. An American MNC executive would be far less ideology- and principle-driven than someone who dedicated over twenty years of his life to fighting for Afghanistan and her way of life.

Whoever the killers, they took away the only force which stood up for Afghanistan and they tore away my life!

Our delegation left for Tajikistan that day, heading for another press-conference in Dushanbe, where Massoud, under heavy guard, once more expressed his satisfaction with the outcome of his meetings. He was greeted by many Afghans who had followed his Europe trip with excitement. When I saw that footage later, I could tell that he was still optimistic and happy.

I myself went to Germany, as planned, to visit my parents for a week and to tick of a rather extensive shopping list of personal supplies, useful items and gifts. Before we parted ways, we were separated from the group for just a minute because the elevator at the airport we were supposed to board was full. So, when we made our way up in the following cabin Massoud said in French so that our two bodyguards could not understand:

"Take care of yourself and come back quickly, o.k.? You know that I need you, right?" He said softly, looking at me from the corner of his eyes.

"I know. I will see you in a week's time." I gave him a brief glance.

With the bodyguards positioned at the door with their backs to us, he found my hand and squeezed it. Without another word we got out and I went to my gate, the bodyguards and Massoud to theirs.

After four years I could see that my parents had aged, after four years of not speaking a word of my mother tongue I had problems forming consecutive sentences filled with only German words rather than Dari fillers or total blanks.

While I was glad to see them, I felt this no longer to be my home after ten years of absence, removed from the culture I was shocked at a few things I saw, things I did not want to deal with any longer. They noticed the change in me and where unhappy about it.

I tried to talk to them about Afghanistan's situation, what the Northern Alliance was and what our goals where, I tried to tell them about Massoud. They did not see my points and thought I was wasting my time. But I guess that only masked their fundamental concern for my wellbeing.

When I flew out of Munich Airport via Frankfurt to Dushanbe, again with an access luggage of almost 70kg, I felt I was going home. When the helicopter landed in Khwaja Bahaudin the following day, the 16th of April, I was home.

The last five months – most precious memories

The last five months of Massoud's life were set against a very hopeful backdrop, which to me added additional tragedy to his assassination. Things were finally looking up.

That year a broad political accord among the often-fractious personalities and factions in the anti-Taliban alliance resulted in an agreement to suspend the activities of contending political parties and focus on co-ordinated military resistance. As a result, over the winter and spring there had been a significant rise in military activity in pockets of anti-Taliban resistance across north and central Afghanistan. Operations in the central region by Shi'a forces during the late winter derailed a planned Taliban offensive against our Jamiat[21] forces north of Kabul.

In addition to Massoud's north-eastern forces, totalling some 12,000, an estimated 10,000 other United Front fighters operated in at least six pockets of territory in the northern, central and western regions of Afghanistan. Loosely co-ordinated guerrilla units were led by the ex-communist Uzbek militia boss Abdul Rashid Dostam, who, after talks with Massoud, returned to northern Afghanistan in April; Shi'a chiefs Karim Khalili and Mohaqeq, whose mainly ethnic Hazara forces had been repeatedly active in recent months around central Bamyan and Yakaolang; and Haji Abdul Qadir

---

[21] Jamiat-e-Islami, the Mujahedin party Massoud was part of

who commanded Pushtun groups in eastern Kunar and Nangrahar provinces. In the west Ismael Khan had returned to boost guerrilla operations in Ghor and Herat provinces, while Atta Mohammad headed forces in the Darrah-e-Suf valley in north-central Afghanistan.

That winter we purchased five used Mi-17 medium-lift transport helicopters which increased our airlift capability to six or seven such aircraft and this had proved crucial in opening new logistics links with allied fronts. Despite the improvement, however, our longer-term offensive capabilities of resistance pockets beyond the northeast seemed constraint.

Our improved financial position was the result of greater control over the mining and marketing of gems. Taxation from the mining of emeralds in the Panjshir Valley and lapis lazuli from southern Badakhshan province had been a source of revenue since the Soviet occupation. However, over the past year Massoud had taken over the lion's share of the gems trade directly and was now marketing both emeralds and lapis internationally.

Yet, the onslaught of the Taliban in Afghanistan and Al-Qaida in other parts of the world intensified.

After the terrorist bombing of the USS Cole in October 2000, in which 17 sailors were killed at Aden, Yemen, the CIA's Panjshir teams tried to revive their plan to supply us with more extensive and more lethal aid. CIA officers sat down at Langley in November and drew up a specific list of what we needed. In addition to more cash -- to bribe commanders and to counteract a Taliban treasury swollen with Arab and Pakistani money – we needed trucks, helicopters, light arms, ammunition, uniforms, food and some mortars and artillery.

We did not need combat aircraft. Tanks were not a priority either.

The list of covert supplies we proposed would cost between $50 million and $150 million, depending on how aggressive the White House wanted to be.

Under the plan, the CIA would establish a permanent base in the Panjshir Valley. Richard Blee, the Bin Laden unit chief at the Counterterrorist Center, argued that the agency's officers had to be on the ground constantly with our men.

The CIA wanted to overcome the confusion and mutual mistrust that had developed with Massoud over operations designed to capture or kill bin Laden. The plan envisioned that CIA officers would go directly into action alongside the Northern Alliance if they developed strong intelligence about bin Laden's whereabouts. In late autumn of 2000, they had sent a memo outlining the CIA's proposal to Samuel Berger, Clinton's national security adviser. But they were worse than lame ducks now at the White House. The November presidential election had deadlocked; White House aides were enduring the strangest post-election transition in a century just as the CIA's paper landed on their desks.

The word went back to the Counterterrorist Center: There would be no new covert action program for the Afghan resistance ...

As the Bush administration finally took office early in 2001, we retained a Washington lobbyist. This lobbyist wrote a letter to Vice President Cheney urging the new administration to re-examine its policy toward Afghanistan. He told Cheney's advisers he knew we could not defeat the Taliban on the battlefield as long as the ruling militia was funded by bin Laden and reinforced from Pakistan. He sought to build up a new political and military coalition within Afghanistan to squeeze the Taliban and break its grip on ordinary Afghans. For this, sooner or later, he would require the support of the United States.

After a while our CIA liaison had slackened, but our intelligence aides still spoke and exchanged messages frequently with Langley. That spring they passed word that Massoud had been invited to France to address the European Parliament. As a result and as outlined above, Gary Schroen and Richard Blee came to meet with Massoud on the 4th of April in Paris.

While the support for the Taliban from Pakistan remained strong Massoud made it a point again and again that continued military resistance to the Taliban remained essential if the Kabul regime were to be brought to the negotiating table and the way opened for a political settlement. Such a settlement, he stressed, should install an interim government - possibly including ex-king Zahir Shah and other neutral Afghans - which should work to collect weaponry, re-establish security and prepare for general elections after one or two years.

The US-government, at the same time, kept rejecting Massoud's repeated accusations that Pakistan was heavily involved with their ISI and regular army forces. They maintained that there was no conclusive proof to these claims.

Only now does it become clear to the world public that Pakistan is less than willing to stamp out the Taliban reminisces in their territory and actively undermine their recurrence. Only now does the US government call for

Pakistan to step up their efforts in this aspect. The acknowledgement of Pakistan's unwillingness to act is a continuation of history as they only denounced the support for the Taliban regime of Kabul shortly before the American invasion. Now that America has been lulled into calling Pakistan a "valuable ally in the war on terror", the reigns have been loosened on the terrorists hiding out in their territory – protected as they were since 1996.

New Delhi

On 20th May 2001 we took another trip abroad: this time to New Delhi, India.

It was Massoud's first time in this ancient country. When we departed, I was very much looking forward to showing him the city, the temples, the historic sites, give him a taste of the colourful beauty of India.

It was a private visit, and he was accompanied by several of his friends and stayed in Massoud Khalili's residence and the grounds of the Afghan Embassy in Chanakyapuri, southern New Delhi. A beautiful, typical old Delhi property with an extensive garden filled with roses all over.

It was just before the Monsoon season, and it had turned already quite warm.

During the first two days in Khalili's house we discussed the political situation and Massoud met with a whole host of Afghans stationed in India. Sometimes it seemed there was a never-ending stream of people. It was more of a casual drop-in situation, so I was always around, met everybody. Massoud introduced me a few times as "being in charge of media relations and civilian projects" other times jokingly as his "General Manager".

After relaxing for one day, we took a trip out of town to Agra, to see the Taj Mahal. The trip was my idea. I wanted to go with Massoud there, to this monument of eternal love.

When we stepped through the south entrance, seeing the Taj "float" on the Yamuna River in front of a perfect blue sky my heart floated just the same. This view never failed to capture me. As we wandered around the grounds, I could see that Massoud was happy – he loved this place just like me. He marvelled at the marble inlay work of the Persian artisans, at every detail of the magnificent building. He was an architect at heart! Always.

Before we drove back to Delhi, I asked our driver to bring us to the opposite side of the Yamuna to view the Taj from there. This is a view not known to many. At the other bank there are camels strolling about with their keepers and local children playing football. When the sun is setting the Taj is painted in subtle pale red, its reflection floats on the calm river. Next to it is a Hindu temple playing evening ragas, and we could hear the sound of temple bells. An Indian picture-perfect opens to those with the love for it.

"I have been to the Taj now for at least five times" Khalili said gazing at the monument, "but I have never been over here. This is absolutely stunning."

"I told you, right, she loves India, she will know these things." Massoud smiled at me, and I knew he would have kissed me now if we had been alone.

At the end of one week, I took it upon me to cook for our party and our hosts North Indian food. Me and Khalili's wife went to the market and got everything fresh. It was a beautiful experience after many months of arid climate and comparatively limited vegetable supply.

That evening we had a feast: Aloo Ghobi, Palak Paneer, Black Dhal, Bindi Masala, Rhaita, Punjabi Saag and Chapati – all vegetarian. To cook this big for ten people I had not done for many years. But I was happy with the results, so was everybody else.

"Where did you learn to cook so well?" Khalili asked

"Oh, you know, I love India – second only to Afghanistan. And when you love something, you want to learn everything about it.

Before I came to Afghanistan, I was engaged to an Indian boy so my prospective mother-in-law taught me many dishes."

"Really? What happened – why did you not marry him? If you don't mind me asking."

"I went to Afghanistan."

"You could have married him still ..."

"Yes, I could have, but I stayed on in Afghanistan and I could not offer him a date at which I would return, so he broke it off."

"You should have married him first. It's not good for a woman to be without husband." Khaliii said half-jokingly.

"I know, but you know, sometimes life is funny. I would love to marry, but what can I say ... Sometimes our emotions get turned up-side-down." I lowered my head and gave Massoud a quick glance. He had been looking at me all the while.

Khalili, who I knew was aware of my relationship with Massoud, kept quiet then, suddenly realising what topic he had touched on.

At that moment his wife stepped in and said:

"Why are you all so quiet suddenly?"

"Oh, nothing really. Ariana just had a thought on the eternal topic of love." He laughed and gave me a wink.

Then we all got up to move to the sofas.

Later that evening I sat outside on the terrace of Khalili's house staring out into the darkness. Only the light of some candles and the chirping of crickets surrounded me. I had left the men in the living room to talk and play a round of chess.

My thoughts returned to the past few days, and I felt so joyful. I then fell asleep, curled up in the big cane-armchair.

After about an hour Massoud joined me, tapping me on the shoulder to wake me up. Sitting down opposite me on the low wall which formed the outline of the terrace he began:

"I did not know that you broke off your engagement because of me. – If I had known I would have not approved of you staying with us."

"So, I was lucky that I did not mention it." I gave him a faint smile

"You love me so much; you have loved me so much from the beginning. I had not given anything to you and yet you gave all your love to me. Only a woman can be like that" he paused with lines crossing his forehead.

"I feel like what I give you is so inadequate compared to what you give me. I was very moved earlier when you told Khalili about your engagement. When he said you should be married, I saw the sadness in your eyes and I felt so bad, so bad about the fact that I can't give you what you deserve: an official expression of my love for you. "

"Oh, no, please don't feel bad. I know why, I know what you are thinking. The only thing that matters to me is that you love me as much as I love you. Just like you have promised me during our first night together – that's it." I emphasised, yet I felt so happy and reassured by what he had said.

"You will never have to worry about that – no matter what. I promise you that again."

"Tell me one thing: if we had met before you were married – would you have chosen me instead?"

"Yes, of course," he said simply, not hesitating for one second. After a minute of silence, he continued:

"If you want me to make you my wife, I will do that – I will take everything on me that results from that. Tell me, please."

My heart jumped to my throat and started beating so loud that I was worried that he could hear it. How I would have loved to become his wife!

"From my emotional standpoint: yes. I would want nothing more. Looking at everything else, I am worried that the price is too high for you to pay. What matters to me is your love for me, nothing else. If a ceremony destroys more than it builds, we should not have it."

He looked at me for a long moment, then nodded.

"Come! Come with me." He got up. "Let's take a walk"

"What about Khalili? What about the other men?"

"Everybody has already gone to bed. And don't worry about Khalili. He is very intelligent and understanding, you know." What he was trying to say was that he knew about us and that he did not object.

So, we left the house, the first and the last time ever in our relationship that we did not try to conceal anything.

We took a walk for about half an hour around the neighbourhood. No one knew us here. There were no problems. Yet we had the Indian guards follow us, just in case.

We walked for some fifteen minutes along the half-dark roads with barely a working streetlight, without saying a word. We passed by many large properties with big trees lining the roads. Rickshaw-walas sleeping in their vehicles, the crescent moon hiding behind the trees.

"I would have never thought that this would happen to me – as if my life is not complicated enough yet." He spoke in French so that no one could understand us. He smiled at me "but I love you so. I can't even tell you. You sooth my soul. You make me happy; you excite me so much."

If the guards had not been there, I would have taken his hand. If this had not been India or any other such country, I would have stopped us in our path, put my arms around his waist and would have kissed him.

When I went downstairs the next morning at nine o'clock the men were already having breakfast, sitting on the floor cushions in the living room.

It was raining and it was very humid. Khalili greeted me.

"Salam, Ariana, please sit. Would you like Coffee, Kawa or green tea?"

I looked at the spread: naan, cream, Indian pharathe stuffed with potatoes and yoghurt. An incredible smell poured from it all. The oil-saturated breads looked yummy.

"Salam – We have Kawa? Yes, please!" I replied. Kawa is a Kashmiri tea made with saffron. It has an exquisitely delicious taste which I never forgo if I get the chance.

As I sat down opposite Massoud I looked at him with a soft smile which he reciprocated. He dipped a piece of bread into the yoghurt. We did not have to say anything. No words necessary. The ceiling fan was humming. The maid poured the Kawa.

After breakfast I left for Afghanistan by myself. The embassy's driver sent me to the airport. Massoud's wife and son were scheduled to join him in Delhi that same day.

So, I left, taking once more only his promise and his love with me. – I had accepted such situations by engaging into this relationship with him, so I had no problem with it. But I had no idea at that point that it would get lots worse in a few months' time!

Yet sitting at the airport I felt lonely, sad. He was right: in a way I had given up everything for him and objectively speaking had not gotten anything in return. But then again, no – I had his commitment, I had his love, despite he would still go through fire for his family – but he would do the same for me, too. He loved me enough to carry on this precarious situation, because, as he had told me he loved me too much to cut me out of his heart, that our bond was beyond everything else, beyond compare. And there was his ring to prove it.

On 25th July a long-time friend of Massoud's visited from France, like he had done several times before. Hashmat Feroz had been a fellow engineering student in Kabul University. During the Russian occupation of the eighties, he fled to France with his family and had ever since become a successful architect there. For several years he had joined forces with a Dr. Paul Lemeut who started various hospital projects throughout the Northern Alliance territory.

It was not a visit characterised by any special events or achievements – it was just friends getting together – for Dr. Lemeut, however, it was a first.

For me this visit has been a deep memory as the dinners and discussion we had were some of the last get-togethers I remember – filled with laughter and joy.

We spoke in a mix of French and Dari. We had tea for hours, just chatting about many things. I remember his face so joyful. Just about a month later he would be dead!

Like many times before I was a focal point in the conversations and as always Massoud was proud to show me off. The two of us joined forces in telling stories. At one such occasion we sat opposite each other in the Astana guesthouse around a rectangular coffee table. While we talked the heads of our guests moved back and forth between us.

When I enjoy people's company, I tend to get quite animated when giving an account. When I got that way Massoud always looked at me with his full attention, obviously entertained and with loving approval of my display. I knew that one of the reasons he was in love with me were my outgoing ways.

Sometimes I got worried that it would become obvious to outsiders what relationship we shared as he would look at me in such an intense way sometimes, caressing me with his eyes. Oh, how exited I would become when I saw the affection pouring from his eyes! How embarrassed I would turn when he - in front of his friends - complimented something I had done!

"How did you like France?" Hashmat asked me

"Oh, I have always loved France, the culture, the language. I studied French in high school in Germany, you know. I went there a few times when I was young and even though now, I have not lived in Europe for over ten years I still love France." I smiled at him "the weather was horrible this time 'round but we were very busy, too, so it didn't really matter."

"Your French is good."

"Thank you. I do manage to speak here with Amir Sahib and journalists."

"I still can't get over the fact that you are doing what you are doing here – I am really impressed. And you have adjusted so well here if I may say so."

"Thanks!"

"I would like to go and see some of your hospital projects – would that be alright?"

"Oh, yes, definitely," I looked at Massoud "perhaps we should go with Amir Sahib so as to make an 'official visit'. See, these are all women related projects."

Massoud nodded.

"We can go to one now" he said "Ariana, do you want to inform Maryam and see whether they are available?" – I sent a messenger over.

And so, we went. It was a bit of a stretch to bring three men to an all-women's hospital and we did not visit the wards.

Familiar with everybody there I was the one explaining things to them.

At one point I disappeared to find one of the doctors and when I returned faster than the men had expected as I did not find her, I caught Massoud saying to Hashmat:

" … She is an incredible woman. Very lovely. At the same time very strong headed and determined." I stopped in my path just before turning the corner.

"You are very lucky to have someone like her work for you." Hashmat replied.

Massoud looked down with his hands in his pockets, then raised his head and looked at me as he saw me walk back in.

"Yes, I am, Hashmat, yes I am" he looked back at his friend.

Hashmat stayed for several weeks, until the end, and also was not spared the pain of a lifetime as he stayed on in Panjshir to work on several construction projects for which he had been planning with Massoud. He like me did not go with him to Khwaja Bahaudin.

Yes, despite the ongoing conflict these last few weeks were filled with beauty, friendship, poetry, and hope − hope of bringing peace to Afghanistan, finally.

Two weeks before the end Massoud moved into his new house. All the family's belongings fitted into one helicopter flight and in no time several men had brought everything into the new building, a spacious two storey house – grand for Afghanistan. It was Massoud's dream house, surrounded by his dream garden. Located on top of a hill, three garden levels and stairs led up to the house. A big swimming pool greeted the visitor who arrived at the top after clearing fruit trees and dozens of rose bushes. But this was not mainly a swimming pool - this was supposed to become a power generator. Like other features of this house showed, Massoud and his architect wanted to be as sustainable and forward-looking as possible.

I was not part of this, I stayed away as much as I could. While he was settling in, he came to see me every day in the Astana. He was so happy to have his dream realise and was full of plans about what he was going to do with his house.

"Finally, all my books will fit into one room. I will start unpacking them today."

He had of course created a library cum office for himself. As I would see in less than a month – when I finally met his wife - the walls were lined with bookshelves there, a desk was facing the window, a sofa bed was there. Oh it was just horrible – too horrible to see this house without him, too much pain, too much, just too much! When I walked up the stairs to the second level and entered his library I broke down, I could not stand it. He had not even gotten around to unpacking all his books, half of the boxes were still unopened.

"Why are you so annoyed and on edge these few days?" he asked me during one of those moving days, while we were

223

sitting in my room in the Astana, and I was signing some papers. The pen I was writing with had run out of ink so – with an annoyed hiss – I pounded my fist onto the table trying to shake leftover ink out of it.

"I don't know" I forced a smile onto my face, then paused.

"You can't bluff me – I know something is bothering you."

A minute of silence.

"I just feel that you have a home now with your family. Where do I fit in now? I don't want to complain, but I still feel sad." I finally said still focusing on that pen.

"What are you talking about? Nothing has changed. All I have done is move. The reason why you feel that way is because you think that I might change my mind and will abandon you. Right? Think about it."

He was right – that was the reason.

"Yah, I guess that's it."

"How often have I told you that I will never do that? How often have I urged you to be with me for the rest of my life? Look at your left hand – I swear to you if ever my feelings were to change, I will ask you that ring back." He said in a very serious, almost upset manner.

"I am sorry. I am sorry" I suddenly came back to my senses and regretted showing such petty feelings "but I love you too much - too much." I looked at him.

"I know" he said in a suddenly soft voice "just trust me, o.k? – I know it must be hard for you sometimes."

"O.k." I smiled at him

"And throw that pen away. From the way it looks even a camel could not extract any more liquid out of it." He laughed. "Come – I bring you to my garden – I will meet Hashmat and his friends there."

224

I had to laugh, too, as I suddenly pictured a camel sucking at my pen.

"Wait" he said as we were about to leave my room "I love you". He stopped me in my path, took my head into his hands and kissed me.

Ever since we had returned from Europe, Massoud had many visitors: journalists, government and NGO representatives, friends.

Some of the meetings, gatherings and tours I attended, depending on who visited, some I would not attend, depending on my own schedule. But if I could at all fit it in, I would make time. The one group of people Massoud did not let me deal with were Arabs – there were few anyway – because he worried that disrespect for me would be in the picture and hence would cause trouble. He knew me too well. He knew that I could not tolerate disrespect neither directed at him nor at myself or anybody close to us. He knew my temper – he called it gracefully 'my passion' – so he did not want to ignite it.

Generally speaking, when there were guests such as journalists, Massoud would of course entertain them, give interviews, and bring them around or simply let them follow his daily life. He was always very attentive to whoever visited, and if he committed time to people, he was theirs. Yet, I would often observe a subtle aloofness in him. Always friendly and kind this was only apparent to someone who knew him well. He appeared somewhat absent to me, with his thoughts somewhere else.

And journalists remained a duty. He did not like to give interviews; he did not like to be photographed. A rather ironic fact, because with his extraordinary magnetism he was a particular draw to filmmakers and photographers. But of course, this resentment spoke to his humble nature. As Christophe de Ponfily once put it: "Massoud will entertain visitors who come to see him, but he does nothing which would encourage them to see him".

Usually, I would be the one making all preparations for the visitors to enter Northern Alliance territory. I would prepare their accommodation and translate interview questions, make all necessary arrangements including their transport, as well as approving or disapproving of certain requests they may have had.

Many visitors were from France. That was nothing Massoud had ever wanted or pushed in any way. It just happened that way because the French tend to take heightened interested in foreigners who speak their language. That is why Massoud received more attention in the French media than anywhere else in the world. All those journalist friends really close to him such as de Ponfilly, J.B. and Rafaele Ciriello were either French or had French connections. Even Hashmat happened to have migrated to France to start a new life. So, there he had started an Afghanistan movement and brought several French politicians to the Panjshir.

In addition, Massoud always had an affinity for the French language, having studied in the Lycee Istaqlal in Kabul. Despite his active speaking skills had decreased somewhat over the last two decades he still understood the largest part of a conversation and even read French poetry.

So, the affinity and connection with France was there, no doubt. It had always been one of the many things which gelled us together – our love for things French. In fact, it was him who introduced me to a few French authors and poets. We also spoke in French most of the time, particularly when we didn't want anyone else to understand.

Massoud always received all visitors with personal attention and hospitality, but to my eyes there always stayed an invisible veil between him and his guests. I believe this veil

227

had probably started to build after his experiences in Kabul and thereafter. How many "friends" had abandoned him after he withdrew his troops from the capital? How many of his commanders had deserted him, bribed away by the enemy, how many had been devoured by twenty years of conflict?

Ever since, I believe, his trust in people had diminished to a minimum. While he had always stayed friendly and open to everybody, no one would know his heart and he would only become totally open to his few close friends.

And he would give total priority to us, too.

I witnessed once the following scene:

I was with him when he received two visitors from the United Nations. I was supposed to translate for him. We were just about to settle down on the sofas. I sat in one corner on the same side as Massoud and the two visitors facing him, when Hashmat walked into the office, unaware that a meeting was taking place. Seeing his friend, Massoud's face lit up, he rose from the sofa and greeted Hashmat bringing him to another corner of the room. The two men had a conversation for some fifteen minutes before Massoud returned.

Here it became clear where his priorities lay: those people who had proven to be his friends and confidants, not those "for whom it is another encounter on their list to meet Commander Massoud", as he once put it.

Most visitors remained journalists. I recall especially the last press conference before Massoud's assassination. It was the 17th of August 2001. We had invited some 15 journalists from 10 international, mostly American, media organisations to Khwajah Bahoudin, all of whom we had not dealt with prior to that. The reason had been to take advantage of the slowly changing tide of public opinion in the US where finally more and more voices demanded of the Bush administration to drop the silent support for the Taliban.

I had had one of the larger buildings emptied for the purpose of the press conference and lined up three tables in the back of the room. This location was most suitable as it provided the most light with its high windows and the most space for the journalists and their entourage.

After the journalists had all settled into their chairs, had placed their microphones on the table and the cameramen had installed their devices, I walked in for a brief announcement:

"Hello everybody. Thank you for coming. I hope you are all comfortable" I began making everybody raise and turn their heads. Not only was their attention shifted from what they were doing at that moment but in most of their faces the inevitable question mark appeared: what is a western woman doing here? While they were aware that I was a woman, by the name Ariana they could not have identified me as a Westerner during our previous contacts.

"Let me introduce myself. My name is Ariana, and I am in charge of media and international relations for the United Front, or Northern Alliance, as most of you prefer to call it. Many of you have dealt with me before. So, I am very pleased to meet you in person. Afterwards we will have the opportunity to meet one on one during lunch.

Please be seated and Amir Sahib will be here shortly after he finishes his prayers"

The journalists all settled down and I began going through some papers I had brought along.

"Excuse me, Miss" Charles Rod from the National Inquirer suddenly spoke up. "I believe I am not alone in my surprise seeing a western woman working and living among the Mujahedin. Can you elaborate on your position?"

"Charles, is it?"

"Yes, correct"

"I have already mentioned my position. That's all there is to it. Everything else is not for public scrutiny."

"How did you end up here, do you have a special relationship with Massoud?"

"Charles, I do not want to elaborate any further. I am sorry. Please respect my privacy. You may pose the same question to Amir Sahib later. If he wants to elaborate, he will."

A moment of silence followed.

Then Antonia Francis from News Week spoke up: "Do you feel it is favourable to Massoud's image in the West that he keeps us waiting just for his prayers? Is he trying to proof a point?"

"Look Antonia" I had to make an effort to hide my irritation, "Amir Sahib does not need to proof any point to anybody except to the people he is fighting for. And certainly, he does not have to make a religious point. He fulfils his Muslim obligations every day whether press conference or not. He has his priorities. But that does of course not mean that he is a religious extremist. You can be religious, moderate, and still a Muslim, you know. Religion in these parts and many other parts of the world is part of people's life. It's not restricted to a once-a-week service. It's integrated in everyday life."

"Why are you wearing a headscarf? You are not a Muslim, right?"

"No, I'm not.

There are certain customs you adopt, religiously rooted customs. And the headscarf is one of them. Part of Indian culture as well, by the way. It is simply part of modest dressing. You would find many Indian women in India still doing the same. And they are from many different religions. Modesty as well as religious dedication is something the West has almost completely abandoned. These things were turned from a virtue into the ways of geeks."

"Does Massoud make you wear what you wear?"

"No, absolutely not. Does your boss make you wear what you are wearing?" I could not resist, prompting subdued laughter from some journalists.

"That's the only comfortable clothing available here. And by the way, I do wear men-clothes sometimes." I winked at her. "And even if other clothes were available, I would still wear this because I enjoy wearing it.

But to answer your real question: Massoud has not forced me to do anything, whatever I do here is out of my free will and I do it with joy. Massoud is the most accommodating man you will ever meet. He is strong and enduring but never coerces others, least of all women. If that were not so I would no longer be here. We all work hard for him because our hearts and souls are in this cause and with him.

Anyway, guys, I think your interest should be focusing on other issues here. There are far more important points for you to make than my dressing, unless someone from Vogue has slipped in without me noticing" I tried to joke, attracting more laughter.

About a minute later Massoud walked in, Jamshid, his personal secretary and brother-in-law in his trail.

"Ladies and gentlemen" I continued "we can start now. Please, everybody who does not speak Dari, Pashto, Urdu or French please direct your questions to me in English, I will then translate them for Amir Sahib."

Antonia was again the first to speak, apparently eager to create a profile for herself.

"Sir, I think I can speak for all when I say that we are all surprised to see a foreign woman working and living here. What is your intension with this? Do you feel it raises your image towards the West – something you have been striving towards for a while now?"

When he set out to reply, he first looked at me with an amused twinkle in his eyes, then turned to the journalist while continuing his answer.

"I do not know whether I should be angry or amused at your question. For the moment I decided to be amused. You see, Ariana is working for us because she has something to contribute. She came with a group of journalists and asked if she could contribute to our cause and, looking at her abilities and dedication, there was a lot for us to benefit from. So, I took her in as a gift from God."

The press conference continued for another hour after which all journalists were treated to lunch.

When I left the room together with Massoud he gave me a half desperate half amused look. "Who are all these people? Will they ever understand us? What else do we have to do over here to overcome their endless suspicions?"

"Well, I told you many times before. Westerners will always be the same: critical and cynical of everything and you have just seen the worst lot: journalists."

One of the non-American journalists was different – he had visited Massoud for the last 18 years every few years to document his progress: Christophe de Ponfilly. He was one of the few Westerners I ever met who had a true love and understanding for Afghanistan. He always said "Je filme c'que j'aime (I film what I love)". He had extraordinary access to Massoud from the beginning and produced the most valuable footage, some of it historic documents. He participated in the above-described press conference, too, but did not ask one single question. Much rather was he waiting for his granted opportunity to interview Massoud alone once more – like he had done many times before.

He did not look at me strange, in fact we got along brilliantly from the beginning when we had met in Paris as we shared the same deep love for the country, her people and culture. Already then, I had explained to him how I had ended up in Afghanistan and he accepted it without much questioning, but heartfelt admiration.

When finally Massoud joined us that afternoon de Ponfilly began with pleasantries – too familiar with the culture. Strangely enough Masoud never seemed to enjoy conversation for conversation's sake even though this is such an integral part of Afghan and Middle Eastern culture. He was too intelligent to put any value to it. He would not be rude, but I could always tell that he was bored.

After a while de Ponfilly got to the point asking me why I was here.

"For the love of this country, her people, her culture, because I feel great pain at their continued struggle. But of course, why I am here is mainly because of Amir Sahib's cause and his vision for his country. I feel very strongly about what has been going on here politically, so I really want to make a difference. Amir Sahib and I think so alike that everything just flows between us – there is not much discussion necessary. "

"Chi gufti?" [What are you saying?]" Massoud enquired in his quiet, manly voice, sipping his tea, sitting cross-legged opposite me.

He looked straight at me over the rim of his teacup and when I told him I could not help but smile. His face, oh his face! I had seen it for almost four years, but it never failed to take me in and mesmerise me.

Though he just nodded, for a second there we were lost in each other's gaze, feeling the deepest affection.

This must have been picked up by Christophe as he asked me later:

"In confidence – there is more to you and Massoud then transpires, isn't there?"

"I can't tell you, Christophe, what do you want me to tell you? Can you keep it to yourself – you are a journalist, you will have to tell, right?"

"No, I won't – I will not hurt a man I admire to the core, for whom I wish nothing but success."

So, he knew, but he did not tell – not now. Only after Massoud's assassination did he talk about me while producing a new interview about his old video "Massoud, L'Afghan" in 2002:

"... He had one secret, one weakness – and her name was Ariana. She was German, living in Singapore and she had come to Afghanistan to work for him in 1997.

After Paris we met again at a press conference in Khwaja Bahaudin on 17th August 2001. That same afternoon I was granted a personal interview with Massoud in his house –

234

and she was there again. This time we were alone – just Massoud, her and myself.

Speaking to me in French. I could now see that she had that same intensity about her like Massoud, some of her gestures even reminded me of him. "Amir Sahib" was in her every other sentence. She was very passionate about his cause and goals for the country, seemed overwhelmed by him – her eyes glowed at every mentioning of his name.

She was the one who served us tea. She served Massoud first, and she knew exactly how much sugar he took, while for me she asked.

She dressed elegantly for the situation she was in, it showed that she did not do the dirty work here, that she was, like Abdullah, the one representing, talking, and arranging.

She explained to me once more why she was here, talking about her love for Afghanistan, her people and culture. You could see that she was completely immersed here, her hand-gestures and other expressions and behaviour showed that.

It was clear, too, that she had achieved a good status among all the men: most notably of course she interacted with Massoud's close circle on an equal basis, she was clearly accepted as such. She would shake hands with these men, while she greeted everybody else without physical contact. For example, before Massoud joined us she told one of the aides to make a phone call to Basarak for this and that purpose. After he was done, he was to bring tea ... It appeared to me that she was viewed as Massoud's right hand, as well as accepted as an authority of her own.

She did not waste many words on such men, neither would she smile a lot. To somebody not familiar with this culture that would have appeared arrogant. But in fact, it was a necessity so as not to appear too friendly with a man and also, in her case, to maintain her authority.

After a while, Massoud, who had been sipping tea, all that while watching her as she spoke, asked her to clarify what she had been talking to me about. When she explained it to him, I could not help but notice that there was an intense connection between the two. Massoud's face showed an affection I had not seen on him before, a forgiving softness which spoke of a different side of him. They seemed to be very close without showing it openly.

I asked her later, and indirectly admitting it she asked me not to reveal anything – with which I complied until now that he is gone.

As far as I know she went to Kabul after Massoud's assassination. She did not aspire to political influence. She had mentioned that several times. So, it was not a case of sour grapes due to the fact that she was a foreigner and a woman.

We, together with some other journalists, tried to get the Massoud Foundation off the ground which aims at promoting all values The Lion of Panjshir stood for and which we felt were going to go under-rated in the years and decades to come, overshadowed by his military legacy."

Christophe de Ponfilly died on 16th May 2006. The circumstances of his passing have not been well published. I learned about it through the internet and was shocked to hear it but nobody at his Interscoop agency could be reached for comment.

Staring at my computer screen tears welled up. He was too closely connected to us all. He was one of the handful of foreigners who really had felt for the country, who had fully understood Massoud and his strive. I felt like another part of my precious memories was ripped from my heart.

Disillusioned and totally heartbroken after Massoud's death he left Afghanistan for two years, saying in an interview that he could not bear to see this country without Massoud and with hordes of analysts descending on it. Analysts who had no knowledge of Afghanistan, judging and commenting, shredding to pieces what was left of it, what was left of this battered land.

I had many e-mail and phone conversations with him after that. We poured our hearts out and discussed what was going on in Afghanistan. I urged him to return and visit me in Kabul. He only did so in 2004 when he had gotten his act back together – at least on the surface.

He wanted to shoot a feature film, called "L'etoile du Soldat" a story about a Russian soldier captured by Massoud's forces. It was completed in 2005.

His scars, however, must have run too deep. So, it has been said that he committed suicide.

Some scars never heal; there is pain that cannot be overcome.

If I did not have my faith, part of which is that I believe that Massoud and I will be re-united after I leave this body, I might have chosen the same path in those horrible past years.

How to lose a dream

"L̶o̶s̶s̶ ..."
You cannot write loss, only feel it"
From "Memoirs of a Geisha"

Big as well as terrible events usually throw their shadows. Some noticeable, some not. Some are too close to be spotted.

It was on 1st September 2001, on a most beautiful Afghan day that I was sitting at the Panjshir River's bank just down the slope from the Astana Guesthouse, enjoying the little breeze which was blowing.

It was about five o'clock when I heard the pebbles behind me squeak; I turned around and saw Massoud; he squatted down next to me without saying a word. I had not seen him the whole day. He appeared in deep thoughts, with lines crossing his forehead.

"Happy birthday"[22] I said, smiling at him.

"Thank you" he smiled back at me, but the smile ran away from his face fast.

I did not ask him anything. We just sat next to each other for a while. Then he said, looking out across the river:

---

[22] It is not common in Afghanistan to celebrate or even mention one's birthday

"I had a dream last night. An old man with a long white beard came to me and told me only these words: 'Enough, Ahmad, enough now.'"

I looked at him – I had heard of the old man before. Massoud had told me once about such a figure appearing to him in his dream when he was young, in 1978. He then had told him to take up the fight against the Communists. He was convinced until this day, that it was God speaking to him. As opposed to the way it has been portrayed in some articles, he was never arrogant about that, never thought of himself as being "a chosen one", he just believed that God had encouraged him to fight for his country.

"If I have to leave you – how will you feel?"

"Please do not talk like that. You drive a knife through my heart!"

"I know that something is going to happen, and if I do not survive it, please do not cry over me." he turned to me with his lovely face, too calm to be real for what he said.

"How do you want me not to cry" I replied with tears already filling my eyes "how can I survive without you, without your love? You promised me never to leave me. If it is God's will now that you must leave, then I want you to take me with you. Please do not leave me here!!"

"I cannot promise you this, my darling. I never promised you anything which I knew I could not keep. I want you to be with me forever. Remember I said: 'I will never hurt you, if I can avoid it with all means in my power.' But some things are out of our hands."

This conversation took place in the last twelve hours I shared with him. The next day, 2nd of September, he left for Khwaja Bahaudin in the afternoon, with me staying behind for one

239

week as there were urgent matters to settle in one of the projects.

Only later did I learn that he hinted his death to his commanders the next day while they were sitting in the garden of his new house in the Panjshir. Ahmad Junior was there as well. Coming up to his father Massoud asked him to run as far as he could up the hill. The boy ran for a while and stopped some hundred metres from the first garden level. When he returned the father said:

"When I die, I want to be buried there, because then I can be sure that my son can easily reach my grave."

After that, caressing his son's head, he continued:

"When I die, I do not want you to cry, I don't want you to have a heavy heart either, because I will have died for what I believe in."

After his father's death Ahmad Junior insisted his father be buried there; but the boy's wish was denied as that way the tomb would have been in a very inaccessible spot, inconvenient for others to visit.

In retrospect I only have one consolation: that same evening we had time to be alone. We met in the guesthouse's lounge at sunset. He ordered tea. I sat in my favourite spot on the windowsill, he on the floor with his back against one of the sofas. Sipping the tea, we discussed the latest military and international situation.

In a silence I turned my head and tried to pierce the darkness outside and the glare of the window with my eyes. Instead, I caught his reflection. He saw that I was looking at him that way. He smiled.

Then he got up and walked towards me. He stopped very close to me, putting his left hand onto the window frame.

"Let's go to your room, shall we? We will not be seeing each other for a few days now."

How cruel these words resound in my memory today. We would not be seeing each other again – ever. The next time I would see him would be in an operating theatre, covered with a white cloth ...

That evening, after they switched off the generator, we went to my room. When we walked in, he casually flung his pakul onto the little coffee table and sat cross-legged on my bed leaning against the wall. I took off my chador and lay down with my head in his lap. He caressed my hair.

"You always have such beautiful hair" he said, "so soft and such a nice dark chestnut colour."

I smiled at him from below. He was slim as always, yet he had broad, manly shoulders. He was fair for Afghan standards, despite all the time he spent outdoors.

He had aged fast in one year, but to me his face had become even more handsome, bringing out his character even more clearly.

After a while he bent down and kissed me. As always, his lips just melted into mine, they always had. I sat up and caressed his cheek – how his beard had turned grey! He never had a very full beard, but that is what framed his face so nicely.

The room was lit up by a kerosene lamp, throwing our shadows against the wall.

God gave us a perfect time that night. I felt such closeness to him, such overpowering affection. Oh, I didn't know that it would be for the last time!

"Stay here with me tonight" I looked at him.

"You know I cannot stay here over night, even though I would love to." He rested his head in his right hand. "I want you to be near me all the time, but you know that we can't." He kissed my shoulder.

I nodded. Putting my arm around his waist I could have stayed like this forever. My face touched his chest, I breathed his scent.

"I will meet some of my commanders later in the morning at my house," he got up, it was 2 am, "and then I will fly back to Khwaja Bahaudin in the early afternoon. The preparation for the offensive is coming to a crucial state and I need to be there.

So, do your work as we discussed and maybe you can be back on Monday already, o.k.?

Oh, and also, these two Arab journalists from Morocco or Belgium or wherever they're from. They have been here now for over two weeks, can you see to it that they come along with me to Khwaja Bahaudin on the same flight, too. I did not have any time to see them so far. I hope I will be able to squeeze in an interview with them there. I believe it would be good if we could demonstrate to the Arab press that there are a lot of Pakistanis and Arabs fighting here."

"Alright, I will make arrangements" I got up from the bed.

He came up to me and held my head, softly kissed me. Then he took my hands.

"I will see you on Monday."

"Inshallah"

He smiled at me, grabbed his pakul off the coffee table, turned around and walked out.

Like a freeze-frame this image is now in my mind - forever.

I had been spared the horrific scenes, which went on in Khwajah Bahoudin that fateful morning of the ninth of September because I had remained in the Panjshir for those few days, as instructed by Massoud. Until today, however, I wish I had been in that room and had died with him.

Instead, that morning I was busy with phoning several people and with quite a bit of paperwork. At around 10.30 I had made my way to Rokha and sat down with Wajiha, the head of the local woman's clinic there, to discuss some issues, afterwards I was scheduled for a meeting in the Emergency Hospital nearby.

Suddenly, shortly after 11.00, I felt a very strong sense of faint and nausea. Even though I was sitting down, I had to support myself by holding on to the wooden shelf next to me. For several minutes my vision became blurred, and, in my hands, I felt a slight cramp. Waving off the attempts by the doctor Wajiha had called to move me out of the chair, I sat motionlessly until the cramp in my hands subsided.

"Are you alright?" Wajiha asked giving me a concerned look "You can't be pregnant ..."

"No" I uttered starring at her "I don't know what this was."

"Is it better now?"

"Yes, it's gone. That was frightening."

"You should get a check-up done. You never know."

Later I learned with shock that the explosives-filled camera, which killed the man I love more than life, went off at 11.10 that morning!

Fifteen minutes later I was done, went for my meeting at the Emergency Hospital and returned to the Astana around midday.

I had sat for fifteen minutes in the living room to go through some papers when the entrance door flung open, almost shattering its glass by hitting the wall. One of our aides stormed in and shouted out:

"Khanum Ariana, please come quickly, something terrible has happened!"

"What??" No answer. "What, for heaven's sake, what?"

When I saw the look on the man's face, I knew that indeed something bad had happened. Instantly terrified I jumped up, scattering all papers onto the floor. Our rudimentary intuition causes such panic because our omni-knowledgeable soul already knows what has happened.

The aide did not want to tell me. The panic increasing inside of me by the second, as we were virtually flying to Massoud's office by car where the satellite phone's handset was lying on the table. I jumped towards the phone. It was Abdullah on the line.

"Ariana" I did not recognise his choked voice, "Amir Sahib has been badly wounded in an assassination attack – those Arabs, remember?"

"Oh God, oh God" I cried out "is he alive?"

"He is, but only barely – I worry he will not make the next hour!"

I sank onto the chair at Massoud's desk, not comprehending what was going on; panic-stricken I dropped the handset onto the table. The aide picked it up and spoke quietly to Abdullah.

"Khanum Ariana" I finally heard his voice from far away. "I'll get the helicopter. It will fly you to Farkhor."

"What about his family?" I asked staring at him.

"No – later"

When I arrived in the Indian Military Hospital in Farkhor right across the border in Tajikistan after the longest two hours of my life, I was beyond myself with hysteria.

Inside this old rattling flying bus, I did not know what to think. I had lost my head, I cried my heart out, thrown into a void the sky outside went by in a daze. I knew that I would not find him alive there, but of course my heart rebelled against this thought to the level of total numbness, clinging to the hope that he would make it.

When I rushed through the hospital entrance I shouted at the staff: "Where is Amir Sahib? Where is he?" They hurried me to the second floor – operating theatre. The first person I saw there was Abdullah and I called out at him "where is he, where is he, how is he ???!" Abdullah stopped me in my path and grabbed my shoulders.

"Ariana, there is nothing you can do" – he looked me deep in the eyes, holding my shoulders tightly and uttered the words I would have killed for to avoid hearing: "Amir Sahib passed away on his way here …" With his words tears filled his eyes and poured down his cheeks.

All I remember at that moment was everything turning black around me – I fainted into Abdullah's arms. When I came to, he was sitting near my bed, his face broken with grief. At first, I had difficulty remembering where I was but then things hit me with double the force.

Still my numb mind did not want to register it. "Where is Amir Sahib?" I looked at Abdullah with desperation, then at the doctor standing at my bed. "Ariana, he is martyred. There was nothing the doctors could do. There were several

246

shrapnel piercing his heart" Abdullah said with a shaky voice. With his words reality hit me: I jumped out of the bed, ran barefooted out of the room and screamed "I want to see him, where is he, where is he?"

At first, they refused me entry to the operating room seeing the state I was in. After I insisted, shouting at the nurse who tried to keep me, they let me pass. When they removed the white sheet from his face my legs gave way and I had to be supported by Abdullah. I was close to fainting a second time. I cried out loud, several times, putting my hands on my mouth. I felt such endless pain, such endless disbelieve, desperation and heartbreak as if someone had grabbed my heart and torn it right from my body. Yet the human psyche is protected from permanent damage by a numb mind, which filters out the toughest reality. His face had not suffered a scratch, only his beard was slightly smouldered, they had washed off the blood. What killed him, I was told, were the small wounds around his chest – the shrapnel which pierced his heart and had exited through his back where he had a ten-centimetre-long wound. His face looked so peaceful, as if he were simply asleep – like I had seen him many times. Just this time the heart, which had reciprocated all my love was no longer beating. I knew that now he was in the peaceful realms of God – but what hell had I been thrown into! Oh God – I can't take this pain. Take me away from here, too, let me follow where he has gone!!

I was in a terrible state, I was beyond myself. It was not grief yet, it was hysteria, still hoping to wake up from this terrible dream.

I wanted to touch him one last time, caress his face one last time. I wanted to hold his body one last time, but I could not – inappropriate it would have been such a public display of affection, even for a wife. But I was not even that – I was nothing, an officially undefined woman in his life. So, I just stared at his face – not comprehending that those beautiful eyes would never open and look at me again.

When they pulled the cloth back over his face and Abdullah took my arm to escort me out of the room I started to scream once more. I could not leave, how could I leave him here, he would have to get up tomorrow, how could I leave him? I crouched down, tumbling with my back against the wall, crying uncontrollably yet again. I slid down the wall until I sat on the floor. Pounding my head against the wall I stared at Abdullah through a curtain of tears. He had squatted down and tried to calm me down. A failed attempt as tears were streaming down his own face.

After a few minutes Abdullah helped me up and we walked out, unable to face the twenty odd people who had by now gathered outside the operating theatre – many of his commanders, everybody. It was the saddest picture. I bent my head, pulling my headscarf over my face. Crying, I walked past all the men, supported by Abdullah.

Until today I have not recovered from a death-wish. If someone could guarantee me to be re-united with him when I leave this body I would want to die today.

Massoud Khalili and Jamshid as well as Fahim Dashty survived the attack badly wounded and burned, not life-threatening though, so they were released from the hospital some ten days later. Khalili could afford to seek further treatment in Germany, accompanied by his wife. He lost sight in one eye. Fahim Dashty went to France to seek more treatment there. After six weeks he flew to London to be interviewed by Scotland Yard about the incidence.

Overseeing media relations, I did remember the two "journalists'" applications and credentials coming through from Wali in London. The truth is all of us were hiding behind somebody else's credentials. Nobody made the effort to investigate on our own. The main assurance probably was the fact that the application was supported by Abdur Rasul Sayyaf.

As it turned out later, however, suspicions fell on him and his Arab Wahabi connections. This is not well investigated until today. Hence, I do not want to support potentially unsubstantiated speculations. It is, however, remarkable that these two virtually unknown individuals managed to get so close to Massoud. This could either point to a straight-forward Al-Qaida involvement or a more sinister elimination plot by outside forces as touched on earlier.

I remember that I found both rather repelling in appearance. As always, intuition should not have been ignored. Because Massoud did not want me to deal with Arabs I did not have much to do with them, a fact which may have contributed to what happened. Maybe I would have had a bad feeling about them, maybe something would have aroused my suspicion, who knows. Instead, I did not speak to them personally anymore after they initially reported to me after their arrival.

I looked at their passports to take their details (all of which turned out to be fake), collected their original credentials, and filed them away.

After that they were hanging around in the Panjshir and Khwaja Bahaudin for almost three weeks simply because Massoud was too busy and before that did not make it back to the Panjshir at the originally intend point in time due to bad weather. People told me later that they were not observed doing any interviews or take a lot of footage. But again, no one became suspicious about this.

In the days leading up to his assassination Massoud was heavily engaged in a counter offensive against the Taliban.

He spent his days and nights pouring over maps, developing strategies and communicating with his commanders, Bismillah Khan leading the operation. – His efforts bore fruits and the enemy could be repelled, ammunition and weaponry seized.

The evening and night before he spent with Khalili. The two friends sat until the early hours reading poetry.

When I spoke to Khalili in Kabul in October 2001, after he had returned from Germany, he told me with tear-filled eyes about the "faal" they had opened from The Diwan of Hafiz that night.

> *'Take out from your heart all the siblings of enmity,*
> *plant the tree and seed of love*
> *Tonight, you two are together.*
> *Valuate, many nights go, many days disappear.*
> *You two will not be able to see each other again'"*

I was shocked and had goosebumps all over my body.

The following is an account of Massoud's last day as told to me by Fahim Dashty, a Kabuli journalist and documentary maker, Abdullah's nephew, a few months after the event and after he had returned from Europe. Dashty had been there to shoot his own footage.

Fahim lived with the mental scares of this experience for the rest of his life until he himself was killed in 2021, twenty years later almost to the date, in the Taliban attack on Panjshir, their successful effort to crush the fledgling resistance which had been scrambled to fend off a second Taliban takeover of the country after twenty years of Western involvement. He could never openly speak of the loss which left a gaping wound in all of us.

"For much of their visit, the journalists stayed in their guesthouse. They rarely went on interviews. They asked few questions. They took little video footage.

One day, Amir Sahib arrived unexpectedly at the journalists' door.

By chance, the two men were away and returned too late. They missed the commander and a chance for their on-camera interview.

Amir Sahib then invited the journalists to accompany him aboard his helicopter back to Khodja Bahaudin. The journalists packed camera and battery pack for the trip.

They were ready to depart when the bodyguards confronted them.

The rickety old Russian MI-17 was overloaded. They would have to stay behind.

The two journalists bumped from the helicopter ended up stuck in Panjshir for two more days. A second helicopter never arrived. Bad weather.

The number of near-misses was beginning to pile up—almost getting into the shura, almost getting Amir Sahib alone at the guesthouse, almost getting aboard the helicopter.

Finally, the skies cleared. Another helicopter arrived to ferry the men to Khodja Bahoudin. They were introduced as journalist guests of Sayyaf.

But, again, the promised interview was delayed. The Taliban-Al Qaeda offensive had begun. Amir Sahib was preoccupied. The journalists had to wait.

They were given a room next door to Gen. Mohammed Arif, who as you know and to add insult to injury, was our chief of internal security.

The journalists wandered through the village of Khodja Bahoudin, killing time awaiting their audience. Two more days passed.

They became familiar figures to the bodyguards. According to them the guards were never alerted to any special threats.

Wali told me earlier, that "a source in Pakistan" warned him about Al Qaeda sending killers "disguised as journalists." He says he passed it along.

But, as you know, reports of assassination intrigues were common. So were foreign journalists."

"You have got to be joking" I interrupted Fahim "it would have been his God-damn duty to investigate in detail – it's his brother for heaven's sake. You don't just pass such things on. You do something about it!!" I was very upset. "Nobody mentioned anything to me either!"

"Yes, absolutely. But nonetheless, Arif claimed this morning that he too was growing suspicious. He says he even tried to stop the interview.

"I told Commander Massoud, 'Please don't meet these two Arabs. Let me arrest them.'"
By Arif's account, Amir Sahib thought about it for two minutes, then said:
'Forget it. These people are just journalists'.

The intensity of a renewed Taliban attack Saturday evening, Sept. 8, caught alliance forces by surprise. Gen. Bismillah Khan feared that his troops might not survive to daylight. At the height of battle, he called Massoud by satellite phone.

Bismillah Khan was especially distressed to advise his friend and commander that a Taliban breakthrough seemed imminent. I heard from an aide later said Bismillah Khan was near panic that night.

Over the phone, Massoud offered encouragement and cool advice on troop deployments. Later, Massoud retired to his quarters with Massoud Khalili. The two men sat cross-legged on floor cushions 'talking about many things— poetry, politics, the situation in Afghanistan,' Khalili told me.

Amir Sahib had an ornately bound volume of the works of Hafiz. According to Khalili he asked him to recite over and over again a favourite verse about friends sitting, talking, enjoying a night like many nights to come, though this night 'will never be repeated.'

The two friends gazed out at the town of Khodja Bahoudin, the stars, the Amu Darya River—until about 4 a.m. Amir Sahib was barely asleep when his personal secretary delivered news that Bismillah Khan's front line had held.

Amir Sahib made his morning prayer, then slept until daylight.

The two journalists learned early the morning of Sept. 9 that finally they would have their audience. It was a sunny day in Khodja Bahoudin as they prepared their equipment.

The interview would be conducted next door, in the bungalow of security chief Arif.

Remarkably, the two Arab men had lived among Amir Sahib's closest and most cautious advisors for more than 20 days, no one knew their real names, ethnic origins or ominous associations.

Affable Touzani was really Dahmane, whose wife still lived with the families of other Al Qaeda agents near Jalalabad. Bakkali was really Alwaer, the taciturn construction worker from Brussels.

The cameraman strapped on his battery pack. He clinched it around his waist.

Over his usual breakfast of tea with bread, cheese, almonds and cream, Amir Sahib received more encouraging reports from his field commanders. He was eager to meet the journalists, to make his case that the Taliban was relying on foreigners—Pakistanis and Arabs.

He then made a radio call to Bismillah Khan at the front in Jabal o Saraj. He asked the general's communications officer if they 'could send up some bodies of dead Arabs by helicopter to show the journalists.'

At the "foreign ministry", Amir Sahib was on the phone again when an aide escorted the journalists into the room. Holding the phone to his ear with one hand, he reached out to shake hands.

At that point I joined them. I set up my own camera and audio gear in the back of the room.

Amir Sahib apologized that this day had been so long coming. Dahmane and Alwaer said they were pleased to meet the legendary leader. They presented their letters of introduction from the Islamic Observation Center in London and its Arabic News International affiliate—the letters ending with: 'May Allah reward you' for any cooperation.

Before the questioning began, Amir Sahib asked Arif to try again to get Bismillah Khan, still hoping to fly some Arab bodies to his camp.

Under any circumstance, such a request would have been difficult. Amir Sahbi's commanders said one of their fellow officers had set up a lucrative trade in selling bodies back to the enemy. It helped finance their war effort. And Arabs, the commanders said in interviews, fetched higher prices than the Talibs because Bin Laden was willing to pay dearly for the corpses of his men.

Amir Sahib sat in a large stuffed chair. Smiling, he slipped off his pakul, and ordered green tea for everyone. They made small talk. What had the men found coming through Taliban territory?

The people are unhappy, Dahmane responded, chatting easily. Arab and Pakistani military men roam Kabul. Omar refused them an interview because television 'is haram'— forbidden under Islamic law. And Taliban ministers were not forthcoming.

Amir Sahib was amused.

I saw for the last time Amir Sahib's smile.

The cameraman calmly set up his equipment in the middle of the room. He seemed impassive, uninvolved with the conversation around him. He adjusted his tripod, set to its lowest level so the camera lens was chest-high opposite Massoud. He asked to remove a small table between them.

Ambassador Khalili, seated on a couch to Massoud's right to help translate, recalled trying to loosen him up before the questions started.

'The cameraman was quite burly,' Khalili recalled, 'and to get the commander in the mood for the interview, I quipped in Persian, 'Is he a wrestler or a photographer?''

Massoud asked to see the interview questions—a list that Khalili then translated for the commander from English into Persian. With that, the Lion of Panjshir turned to the camera and said: 'You can start filming now.'

I was still adjusting my camera, trying to compensate for backlighting from a window behind Massoud.
Dahmane started to ask the first question. Alwaer switched on the camera.

Khalili said 'blue, thick fire' rushed at him—and he heard a 'poof.' His teeth clenched.

He said he heard a voice inside telling him that this was his final moment. 'Then I started screaming, 'God is great!'' And he lost consciousness.

I jumped in surprise at the flash of light, thinking that my camera had malfunctioned. Then I felt a burning all over my hands, legs and face. I rushed out of the room.

Returning I run up to him. 'What happened to Commander Massoud' I gasped.

That's when I looked back at the room for the first time. I saw fire, smoke, dust, smashed windows, broken furniture. The room was destroyed. I smelled gunpowder.

The bomb in the battery pack had blown the body of cameraman Alwaer in half. But Dahmane had only minor cuts from flying glass. He tried to run from the scene, muttering that he didn't know what happened. Security officers locked him in a room. When he escaped through a window, he was killed.

Haji Mohammad Omar, Amir Sahib's bodyguard for 12 years, rushed inside. Everything was on fire. He found Massoud still seated in the armchair, surrounded by devastation, his face and body covered in blood.

Amir Sahib whispered: 'Pick me up.'

At Jabal-o-Saraj, Bismillah Khan and his people had prepared a large meal for Massoud and his entourage. They were expected for lunch after the interview. No one arrived. No one called to explain. The general picked up his satellite phone and called Khodja Bahoudin. No one answered.

At Massoud's camp, it was a four-minute drive from the "foreign ministry" to the airstrip. Omar, the bodyguard, held Massoud in the backseat, the commander's head on his lap. He was still breathing as they bounced toward the helicopter pad, but blood poured from his thigh. And as they pulled up to the aircraft, the bodyguard knew that it was hopeless.

'Amir Sahib has stopped breathing,' he said.

Ambassador Khalili faded in and out of consciousness. Once airborne, he revived briefly, he recalled.

'I saw my commander's face and thought to myself, 'He's dying and I'm dying.''

Everyone was quiet. The only sound was the helicopter rotors.

The rest is known to you."

I listened with tear-filled eyes. But then he added something, which made me cry out:

"Ariana, Omar mentioned something else which I haven't told anybody so far.

When he carried Amir Sahib to the helicopter, he thought he heard him say 'Ariana!'. But he said he couldn't be sure."

Could his last word in this life have been my name??!

The other woman

It took me until the 20th of September 2001, five days after his body was laid to rest, to round up the courage to approach Jamshid with the request to introduce me to his sister Sediqa. Massoud called her Pari. I finally wanted to express my condolences to Massoud's wife. I wanted to confront the situation which I was conveniently able to avoid for four years.

Sadiqa is the daughter of Colonel Dost Mohammad Khan's (Massoud's father) uncle, a man they called Kakar Tajjudin. So, she was Massoud's cousin once removed. It was of course an arranged marriage as it is custom in Afghanistan. Men and women are not at liberty to mix directly. There are no love-marriages in the western sense of the word.

She must have gone through hell, like me. Worse, for days she was not allowed to see his body – for security reasons, they told her. Modesty commanded that she remained in the background at the funeral, her son Ahmad bidding farewell to his father instead.

I attended the funeral from a distance, too.

When they unloaded his coffin from the helicopter all the heartbreak, all the endless pain collapsed on top of me, and I started to cry uncontrollably.

There must have been a crowd of twenty thousand people gathered to attend the funeral procession from his village to Saricha, where he was to be buried. – His coffin was loaded onto a flat-bed truck. His father-in-law, Tajuddin, Ahmad and many others of his close affiliates and relatives rode along. Sayaf was there, Abduallah, Rabbani and many more.

It was a risky endeavour. With all of the valley focused on the funeral and most of the resistance leadership in one spot, the crowd could have easily been attacked in a summary execution. So many eyes scanned the sky ever so often.

When the helicopter had landed the crowd pressed forward, all wanting to be close to him for the last time. As a result, they were unable to open the loading bay of the helicopter. Abdullah, standing at the door, with tears pouring down his face shouted at the crowd to back off.

It took several hours for the precession to reach Saricha. I went ahead with my driver and waited there, sitting in the shade of his office building.

After they had carried the coffin to its final resting spot I backed out from the crowd – anyway that is where the exclusive male domain began with prayers at his grave. But aside from that I just wanted to be alone – this pain was too much for me to bear. I walked, stumbled rather, from there down to the river, crying my heart out – it took me some fifteen minutes to reach the bank. I sat there for two hours just staring into the waters, up the mountains – peaceful and quiet, not paying respect to the turmoil in my heart. – This was his land, his beloved Panjshir!

And I was completely alone. Who would ever comfort me? No one thought of me as someone more affected by this tragedy then the rest of them. I had no home to go to, just my room in the guesthouse. And everything had fallen apart!

"Stop all the clocks, cut off the telephone,
Prevent the dog from barking with a juicy bone,
Silence the pianos and with muffled drum

261

Bring out the coffin, let the mourners come.

Let aeroplanes circle moaning overhead

Scribbling on the sky the message 'He is Dead'.

Put crepe bows round the white necks of the public doves,

Let the traffic policemen wear black cotton gloves.

He was my North, my South, my East and West,

My working week, my Sunday rest,

My noon, my midnight, my talk, my song;

I thought that love would last forever: I was wrong.

The stars are not wanted now; put out every one,

Pack up the moon and dismantle the sun,

Pour away the ocean and sweep up the wood;

For nothing now can ever come to any good."[23]

[23] H.W. Auden, Funeral Blues

When we walked up the three flights of stairs leading up to Massoud's new house, Jamshid still having difficulties walking with various bandages covering his body, I felt like I was walking to my execution. Aside from the endless grief and sadness which had taken possession of my heart I now also felt guilt of sorts. When we walked through the door at the back end of the two-storey house Parigul had already prepared tea in the living room. Her eyes were painfully bloodshot, and I could see that she was going through the same trauma as me. What an awkward situation: the wife and the lover meeting over the death of the man who meant the world to both.

She was my age, born in 1970, just one year older than me. She had green eyes like me, was fair as me, but despite her age she appeared to be no older than twenty measured by Western standards of maturity. When she spoke to me, I felt she spoke to an older sister, respectfully and sweet. At the same time, she was much more of a woman than I was. She had been raising six children, I had not even had the experience of giving birth, she had experienced suffering, which I had no measure for. Still, observing her I understood what Abdullah meant when he had told me: "you can give him things his wife can't give him. You can match up with him intellectually and at the same time give him the thrills of a beautiful woman. That he has never experienced."

Given this situation and prepared for the worst I was totally taken aback by what happened next: When she saw me entering with her brother, she came up to me and hugged me, holding on to me for several long seconds. The tears rushed to my eyes, I embraced her just the same. "I have come to express my condolences to you! This is an awful, awful time for all of us!" – I have never been good at finding the appropriate words when confronted with suffering and pain.

"Please sit" she said pointing to the floor cushions, wiping away tears. I did not know what to say.

When I reached for the tea kettle to pour her tea, she saw the ring Massoud had given me.

"This is a beautiful ring – where did you get that from? It is lapis, isn't it?"

"Yes, it is. I bought it once in Singapore. They actually said that the stone was from Afghanistan ..." I lied to her, unable to hurt her even further.

I was even more shocked to hear what she said next:

"Amshira, ("sister", a common way to address a woman of similar age by both men and women)" she began "I am very happy to finally meet you. I have heard so much about you and all the work and effort you have put in for Afghanistan and for my husband. You being a foreigner, that's unbelievable. Everybody speaks so well of you."

"I ..." I tried to say something meaningful, but she interrupted me:

"No, please, I have to say this: you have made my husband very happy; I know that. You have kept his company through thick and thin, near the frontlines and everywhere. Everywhere where I could not be with him, which was in most places. You were his support, his mental strength where his own failed, his soulmate and more. I have known about it. Do not worry about that, do not apologise. It was a good thing - that."

She paused, her eyes filled with tears, and I was once again lost for words. All I could do at this moment was to move over to her and hug her again.

"I am sorry" I finally said letting go of her "but sometimes there are things in life we have no control over."

That applied for all of us concerned: she had no control of her husband's extra-marital relationship, Massoud and I had no control over the strongest of feelings which had besieged us.

With that of course I knew that she had been aware of our relationship. As a woman she must have known, I did at no point consider her naïve. However, I doubt that Massoud ever spoke to her openly about me, it was probably left to her to put one and one together and then decide whether or not to accept it. The fact that she accepted it can mostly be attributed to the fact that men in Afghanistan still are the ones with choices, while women are not.

Even though Massoud moved at the fringes of societal acceptance by having this relationship with me, yet not marrying me, his status and reputation among his people but also – and mainly - our discreetness allowed this to carry on.

At the same time, I believe she spoke the truth when she said she appreciated my support for her husband in the various levels of his struggle. She succumbed to the fact that he and I had a connection they did not share but knowing her husband and his needs she knew why he was attracted to me.

As a result, we did not become girlfriends, but I was glad to have left a friendly situation behind rather than a sour one.

Soon after that the family moved to Iran, their whereabouts kept strictly confidential.

I have not heard from Sediqa ever since.

Epilogue

As the bombs fell on Afghanistan from 7th October 2001, when the US-led invasion of the country began, we only slowly realised what had happened.

On September 11th, 2001, the "horror without comprehension and endurance"[24] had struck the United States with the attacks on the World Trade Centre. The evil which their government had let ferment in the region, against all Massoud's warnings, had found a target.

As the world watched in horror and the US government planned their invasion of Afghanistan like a bull stung by a hornet, we sat grief-stricken by Massoud's death and overwhelmed by the powers unleashed onto Afghanistan. We realised that the country had become the target of revenge because the Taliban was accused of having harboured Bin Laden and his posse.

After five years of strife and tribulations Massoud's first goal was about to be realised with the help of the Northern Alliance: the ouster of the Taliban regime. But it had pleased God to call him away only a few weeks before. A poignant tragedy!

So, it was a bitter-sweet victory for us. Massoud was no more to savour it and take a stake in the formation of a new Afghan state. – Instead Fahim Qasim had been designated

---

[24] Ahmad Shah Massoud, Strasburg, April 2001

Massoud's successor and led the military take-over of one Afghan city after the other.

In the Bonn Conference in December 2001, following the de-facto take-over of the country by Northern Alliance and NATO troops, Hamid Karzai was appointed President of an interim Afghan government and Fahim its defence minister.

As for me, I stayed on in Panjshir until the middle of October, when I went to Kabul to join J.B. in starting his photography and film-making NGO in the heart of the city. The compound was big enough to provide accommodation for me.

As the months went on and the political situation started to calm down, I began shuttling up and down to Panjshir to continue with the civilian projects I had been overseeing with Massoud. Those were part of his legacy and deeply meaningful to me.

So were all the grassroots contacts I had made over the years which I managed to keep to this day. I stayed away from the political circus, instead trying to continue to make a difference for the people on the ground with both hands-on work as well as fundraising.

These activities superficially covered the gaping wound his death had left in my heart. But of course, it took only the slightest rattling and it burst open again.

I spent hours at his tomb whenever I was in Panjshir, sitting by the hastily filled up mound, covered in flowers. It remained a make-shift tomb until 2004 when they started building a small white dome with a green roof. Modest and befitting his character. Only 2010 saw the construction of the marble-glad structure which is there today.

The past four years had forever changed me.

Since the death of the man, I love more than life itself, a shadow has been following me, a cloud of quiet sadness which I can't get rid of.

In the beginning, when I finally started to sleep better at night, I spent much of my days indulging in memories, collecting photographs, writing things down, daydreaming, crying. Especially in the winter of 2001/02 there were days when my curtains remained drawn all day. A city without power, cold short winter days and snow-covered streets didn't help.

He had become an addiction, a drug, which needed ever higher dosages. It was like trying to fill a bottomless pit. A destructive mental state to be in because it can only end in an over-dosed mind. Seeing myself heading for this abyss, by the grace of God, I managed to pull myself back from the brink by throwing myself into work. There was also drinking, and partying involved, hanging out with the many foreigners who started pouring into Kabul and in the process had opened several watering holes in rather quick succession.

But in the end, towards Christmas of 2002, things calmed down as my life in Afghanistan moved me forward and I put all my energy into working for his memory and for his dreams.

I locked my love for him into a shrine in my heart. Untouchable and sacred. And this is where I am today.

Somewhere beyond right and wrong,
There is a garden.
I will meet you there.

Rumi